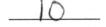

Dave Hutchinson

A special signed edition, limited to
200 numbered copies.

This is number:

_10_

The Push

The Push

Dave Hutchinson

With an introduction by
Eric Brown

NewCon Press
England

First edition, published in the UK November 2009
by NewCon Press
41 Wheatsheaf Road, Alconbury Weston, Cambs, PE28 4LF

NCP 20 (signed hardback)
NCP 21 (signed softback)

10 9 8 7 6 5 4 3 2 1

ISBN:

978-1-907069-08-6 (hardback)
978-1-900679-09-3 (softback)

Cover art and design by Andy Bigwood
Book edited by Ian Whates

Book layout by Storm Constantine

Printed in Great Britain by the MPG Books Group,
Bodmin and King's Lynn

Introduction

By Eric Brown

Dave Hutchinson, Hutch to his friends, has been on the SF scene now for over three decades. In the Seventies, in his precocious late teenage years, he sold four collections of science fiction stories to Abelard, straightforward genre tales which even at that early age displayed a grasp of story-telling way beyond his years. These days he dismisses the books as juvenilia – and will probably be embarrassed by their mention here – but the fact is that even back then he was writing stories grounded in the principle objectives of fiction: to tell interesting stories about interesting people in a marvellously readable and compelling way.

Now, some thirty years later, Hutch is still telling marvellously readable stories, but as is to be expected he's grown, expanded his repertoire and honed his techniques. He understands more about the art of storytelling, and also about science and psychology – and the result is a string of stories that are among the best that the genre has to offer.

The question I ask myself, when considering his standing in the SF world, is why Dave Hutchinson is not more acclaimed. Among the cognoscenti his name is a by-word for excellent literary SF, but to the general reader he's relatively unknown. Well, perhaps that's because he's hardly prolific. In 2002, Cosmos Books published *The Villages*, his only novel to date, and in 2004 his collection *As the Crow Flies* was published by BeWrite Books. The collection, in my opinion one of the best to come out of the genre in recent years, contains story after brilliant story which not only fulfil the criteria of all top-flight fiction, great ideas and penetrating insight, combined with fine prose and deft plotting, but also say something about the human condition. In a genre that prides itself on cutting edge ideas, and often values content over form, Hutch manages to combine original ideas with penetrating human insight. Two stories in particular stand out, "Discreet Phenomena", a surreal fantasy which fuses the supernatural and the naturalistic to striking effect; and "The Trauma Jockey", a noir SF tale about the consequences of having the ability to take on the pain and angst of others.

So… two books in recent years: not exactly productivity of Silverbergian proportions; which is perhaps the reason Hutch is not as well known as he should be. He's a journalist by trade (this perhaps shows in the honed precision of his language) and in recent years the day job has taken precedence over his creative output. Another reason he isn't up there with Baxter, Hamilton and Reynolds is that he writes literary SF, and rarely ventures into the territory of space fiction about colony worlds and aliens and starships on the edge of known space.

In recent years, however, he's been gaining a growing reputation: his stories have been taken up by Ellen Datlow and published on the prestigious SciFi.com website, and he's placed stories with Interzone and various anthologies.

The publication of this novella, *The Push*, will further

enhance his reputation.

It is core genre stuff, and Hutch shows that he can not only write space opera – or planetary romance, or whatever you care to call SF set in space, with starship and aliens – but can do so with the best in the field.

The central conceit is great – an idea that would sit centre stage in many a science fiction writer's work, but Hutch uses this as the mere backdrop to a far larger human story involving a neat use of Einsteinian time-dilation, the ethics of colonisation, corporate intrigue and much more. At the centre of the narrative is prickly, sardonic Neil, a co-discoverer and founder of Reith, and his reluctant return to the colony after more than two hundred years to investigate the evolving situation. In the course of the story we learn the reason for this reluctance, and it's this, the human element of *The Push*, that is the story's main delight, as you will soon find out.

Dave Hutchinson is a fine writer, much undervalued; with this novella he will, if there's any justice in the world, find a wider audience.

Eric Brown
September 2009

One

When I was very young – this was before interstellar travel – popular culture used to call the place a spacecraft was controlled from *the bridge*, and *the bridge* was usually at the front of the spacecraft. And quite often it would have big windows, so you could see the stars and planets and all that really cool stuff. The ships were also interesting metal creations, sometimes sleek, sometimes hairy with antennae of indeterminate purpose, and lots of *windows*. I mean, *really*. There are easier ways of doing things.

The *Wednesday Addams*, the boat I hired to get to Reith, was carved out of a battered ball of rock about three kilometres across, a mined-out castoff from the Belt, its heart spongy with corridors and caves where freefall miners had extracted valuable minerals and metals. Its pilot, a bandy-legged little Australian rasta named Gideon, was going to be paying the mortgage on its fusion engines and Push motors for a very long time, but he seemed in no great hurry. It had no windows, and all its antennae were sunk into deep pits to protect them from micrometeorite strikes. As Gideon usually travelled alone, there was no need for a *bridge* as such. He'd simply installed all his control room equipment in his living quarters, which were right in the heart of the rock and stank of dope and patchouli and joss and were plastered with posters of Bob Marley and the Emperor Haile Selassie and views of the Great Barrier Reef. There was also a big spherical tank full of koi carp. Gideon – and indeed the carp – seemed to prefer zero-gee, but I could never sleep in free-fall so he'd reluctantly fired up the centrifuge which contained the seldom-used passenger compartment. It only provided a fraction of a gee, but at least I could get some shuteye. You get to my age, sleep starts to be important.

***

We were five hours out of the Push when Gideon's voice came over the intercom. "Hanson, mate," he said. "You want to see your *destination?*"

I didn't really want to see anything. The trip had taken three months and, eventually bored out of my mind, I had decided to spend the latter part of it in suspension; Gideon had only woken me up a couple of hours before we came out of the Push and I was still hobbling about like a thousand-year-old flu victim. Cursing under my breath, I pulled on a sweatshirt and a pair of shorts and drifted gingerly through the maze of rooms and corridors down to Gideon's quarters.

Although he maintained a veneer of almost outrageous cool, I thought Gideon might be a tiny little bit overawed by me. It was unusual for private individuals to charter Push boats. Governments, certainly, if they had the need. Corporations, absolutely, if they needed to freight something somewhere in a hurry and all their other boats were in transit to somewhere else. Companies, sure. Individuals, no. In cash? Never. I had toyed with the idea of telling Gideon just how much interstellar travel had cost, once upon a time, but I didn't want to blow his mind.

In his cluttered rooms, Gideon sat, surrounded by consoles and monitors, in an enormous overstuffed oxblood leather armchair that looked as if it had come from a fire sale at a gentleman's club. He waved me in through the door and pointed at a big monitor on one wall, on which a little blue and white ball floated on a depthless field of black.

"Super," I said, and turned round and went back to the passenger quarters.

***

I was feeling better the next time I visited. Reith almost filled the screen and Gideon was busily typing on a couple of touchboards at once. I stood behind his armchair and looked at all the readouts. Someone once told me that Reith had a tricky orbital approach, but it looked fine to me.

"Doesn't Reith have a tricky orbital approach?" I asked.

Gideon glanced up at me. "You what?"

"Reith," I said. "Tricky orbital approach."

Gideon shrugged. "Not so's you'd notice." Still typing with one hand, he held out a headset. "Man wants to talk with you."

I put on the headset. "Hello?"

"You're here," said Sheldon.

"No," I said, "I'm here. *You're* there."

There was a moment's silence. "Yeah," he said. "Granddad warned me about that."

"About what?"

"Your sense of humour."

Gideon had stopped typing and was following my side of the conversation, a broad grin on his face. I said, "This is not the first time my reputation has preceded me."

Sheldon said, "Man, you have no *idea* what has preceded you. See you soon." And he hung up.

Reith had a new moon. It was fifty kilometres across and an almost invisibly-thin line of silver light tethered it to the planet, disappearing and reappearing as we changed position relative to the sunlight coming from Reith's primary.

"Overlook Station," Gideon said as the lumpy agglomeration of modules and solar wings expanded steadily on the main screen. "Li'l Babylon."

I walked over and stood in front of the screen. I leaned down close and tried to focus on the silver line. "Space elevator?"

"Skyhook," Gideon said with a snap of distaste in his voice. "*They* call it *The Hook*."

"Wow," I said. Technology on Reith *had* come on since I last visited.

Gideon snorted. "Babylon be Babylon, I an' I say, mate."

***

We docked at Overlook. I did the immigration thing, which took about a minute and a half. I paid Gideon. He tried to say goodbye with a handshake routine that was too complicated for me, so we settled for exchanging eddresses and I wandered off through the bustling modules of the station.

Wearing grippy-soled slippers that made me move like a faintly psychotic mime in the low-gee, I walked down broad shop-lined boulevards, through bustling crowds of people dressed in everything from utilitarian olive coveralls to floaty panes of silk and chiffon. Nobody spared me more than a passing glance, which was how I liked things. I noticed a lot of the big franchise chains among the shops, which I liked a little less.

I walked on. Lines of lindens ran down the middle of the boulevards; sparrows perched on the branches. The air smelled fresh and piney. I hoped Reith hadn't become decadent; I knew that would really annoy me.

I walked to a transit station, got on the first train that came in, put my card in the ticket slot and typed for Central. I took my card out of the slot, stowed my tote in the overhead rack, and sat on one of the lubriciously comfortable bench seats for the seven-minute ride.

Sheldon was waiting for me on the platform when I got off the train. "I didn't meet you at the dock," he told me.

"There are some places where that might be considered unfriendly," I said.

He did a little double-take, but he recovered quickly. "I thought you might want to walk around a bit," he told me.

I looked at him. He was about eighteen years old, Reith, which made him twenty or twenty-one, Terran. He had a plain, flat-featured face and short brown hair. He was wearing a pair of jeans and a long white collarless shirt, and he was barefoot and hanging onto a grab loop that hung from the station's low ceiling. "I've walked around a bit," I said.

"What did you think?"

"Babylon be Babylon," I told him.

That didn't faze him for more than a second. "Is that all your luggage?" he asked, nodding at my tote.

"All the important stuff," I told him. "Where's Raul?"

"Granddad doesn't get up to Overlook very much these days," he said. "He doesn't get anywhere much, these days." He was looking at my face with what I thought was undue interest. "I don't know what he's going to think of *you*."

"That happens to me a lot."

"I can imagine. Okay. Shall we go?"

***

What was, from a few million miles away, a nearly-invisible thread, was actually a structure of woven diamond composite a

15

kilometre wide. Overlook Station sat atop it like the knob on the end of a very long walking stick. Except the walking stick poked all the way down from orbit, through a suborbital counterweight, and into Reith's atmosphere. Dozens of elevator cars ran down the hollow interior of the Hook, each the size of a railway carriage stood up on end. For the first couple of hours motors drove the cars down the shaft; then gravity took over, the motors disengaged, and for the next three hours they dropped in freefall. Some of the more seasoned travellers floated about, chatting and taking advantage of the car's refreshment facilities, but apart from toilet breaks I stayed strapped in for the whole trip, even when the gravity brakes cut in and we started to slow down into the terminal. Some maniac had decided it might be a good idea to install windows in the cars. Looking out, it was like falling down the inside wall of an infinitely-long pipe, and I didn't like that at all.

The Hook was anchored to one of the countless little islands that almost circled the equator in a straggly archipelago thousands of miles long. I remembered flying over it once, naming the islands at random after ex-girlfriends, ex-wives, long-dead pets, characters in favourite novels, memorable meals, entire football teams. I remembered John-Jakob sitting beside me in the cockpit of one of the little vtol aircraft we'd brought with us, noting each name down on his palmtop and giggling maniacally because I had finally got into the spirit of the whole enterprise. I got so far into it that I took the jet off autopilot and almost crashed us into the sea in my eagerness to take a close look at my new realm.

The elevator was anchored deep in bedrock. It seemed to erupt out of the ground and just kept on going. Outside the terminal, the breeze brought scents to me that I thought I had forgotten. I'm not a student of seas, but Reith's oceans had a smell all their own. I slung my tote over my shoulder and looked back at the Hook. You couldn't follow its course up very far without lying flat on your back on the ground, and the overcast cut off the view anyway, so there was no point. I thought it must be a magnificent sight, at certain times of the day, from certain angles, at a certain distance, but my sightseeing days were long past.

"Babylon," I murmured.

"Beg pardon?" asked Sheldon.

I looked at him. He had a smooth, innocent look that I didn't entirely trust. He was Raul Marquez's descendant, after all. "Which island is this?" I asked.

"It's called Sharon-Mae," he said. "Nobody knows why." He started to walk down the wide boulevard of poured stone that led from the terminal to a little town arranged around the smooth curve of a bay in the middle distance.

I stood where I was. *Sharon-Mae.* You should never name things after ex-wives. Particularly if there's an even chance of you outliving them by a couple of hundred years.

"What do you mean 'nobody knows why'?" I said, hurrying after Sheldon.

***

When I left Reith the last time, Jakobstown – the rather grandly-titled Planetary Capital – comprised a hundred thousand or so generic-looking nanospun buildings situated with nitpicking neatness on the left bank of the Slow River on the West Coast of the continent we had decided to name Home.

Seventy years on, Jakobstown stretched into the distance, a neat, tidy, planned march of yellow native stone and wide streets and discreetly-segregated industrial zones and huge parks.

"You guys have been busy," I said, not without some admiration. Two hundred or so years ago, this had all been fertile river-bottom land, nothing but birds and half a dozen species of

17

herbivore we couldn't be bothered to name, too stupid to even raise their heads from munching the grass as we shot them for food.

Sheldon looked at me. "Pardon?" He glanced out of the jet's window. "Oh." He seemed almost embarrassed. He'd looked like that a couple of times on our journey down the throat of the Hook, when we had managed the semblance of a conversation. "This is really weird for me," he said. "You'll have to forgive me."

"You're forgiven," I told him.

"I mean," he went on, "we studied you in school and everything."

"Just don't go crazy on me, Sheldon," I said.

"Right." He pulled himself upright in his seat. "Right. No problem."

A limo was waiting for us at Jakobstown's airport. I had stopped trying to remember Reith the way it had been, on grounds of survival. It was too much of a shock; too much had changed. I had decided to treat the place as if I was arriving for the first time.

"Los Angeles," Sheldon offered as we walked across the spotless marble floor of the airport's arrivals building through the throngs of travellers on their way to other cities, other continents.

I looked at him.

"Granddad's idea," he said. "He wanted Jakobstown to look like Los Angeles in the 1930s. You know?"

I shook my head. I had only been to Los Angeles once. Half the city had been under martial law. The other half had been composed of towers and spires that, in retrospect, might have been aspiring to Hook status.

"Granddad's got this old architecture book," Sheldon said lamely.

I looked around the terminal as we walked, and this awed

little voice began to whisper right at the very back of my mind. *Jesus, we actually did it,* the voice said. *We built a bespoke civilisation.*

***

An hour's drive in the limo took us into the low rounded hills that overlooked Jakobstown to the North. At the head of a long, narrow, neatly-wooded valley was a big red-brick house with a slate roof. I recognised the place instantly; I'd first seen it more than three hundred years ago. Raul had built himself a replica of the house where he was born.

So I knew before Sheldon opened the front door that there would be a big hallway with a wood-block floor and a wide oak stairway with brass carpet rods, and five shiny black panelled doors with brass handles leading into the dining room and the lounge and the stairs down to the kitchen and Raul's Dad's study and the cupboard where the cleaning equipment slept. I didn't even bother to let Sheldon show me the way; I went straight to the study door, turned the handle, and opened it.

Inside, sitting in a life-support chair, was a very *very* old man.

"Hi, Neil," said the very very old man. He frowned. "Is that all your luggage?"

***

Modern medical science is a wonderful thing, but Raul was a hundred and forty years old and everything has its limits.

"You're looking well," I said.

He laughed. "I look like shit. And this is one of my good days." He reached out and took my empty glass. His chair glided noiselessly across the study to the bar and he poured us both another vodka and tonic. "This is what happens when people live too long. Let this be a lesson to you." He brought my drink back and handed it to me before manoeuvring himself back behind his desk.

"Granddad turned down a spinal graft," Sheldon said from his chair in a corner of the room.

"Because the best odds of success the doctors could give me were thirty-seventy," Raul said, gesturing with his glass. "And a forty percent chance I'd wind up quadriplegic." He shook his head. "No thank *you*."

"What happened?" I asked.

"Riding accident," he said. "Down on the West side of the estate. Horse put its foot down a rabbit hole and threw me." He looked sad. "Horse broke its leg. Had to shoot it, of course." He looked at me. "Remember when we'd have done anything to keep a horse alive?"

I nodded. We had brought fourteen thousand frozen fertilised horse ova with us from Earth, but for some reason we lost most of them when we tried to thaw them. It had been touch and go for a while if there would ever be horses on Reith. The rabbits, of course, had come out of suspension without any problems. Now I thought about it, I'd had the bright idea of bringing them in the first place. Probably not a good time to remind anyone about that. I sipped my drink and winced slightly. Raul still made his drinks strong.

I said, "Don't you have advanced equine medical facilities here, then?"

He didn't answer. He was looking intently at me from behind the desk. All his hair was gone, and his skin was the colour and texture of old parchment. He appeared to be slowly mummifying, but his eyes were as bright and alive as I remembered. From my point of view, I had last seen him three years ago. From his point of view, he had last seen me seventy years ago. We could have spent all night discussing the philosophical angles of this, but I suspected that this was not why he had asked me to come here.

"Where have you been?" he asked.

"Lots of places," I said. "The Dependencies. Daybreak, Nowa Polska."

"Pictoris?"

"I looked in."

"How was it?"

"Habs everywhere. The whole system looks dandruffy with them these days. You wouldn't recognise the place."

He took a swallow of his drink and put the glass down in front of him. "You came in on a commercial boat."

"I don't have any boats of my own any more."

"Yes." He touched the surface of the desk and an A4-sized sheet of pearly blue light appeared in the air before him. I could see lines of writing scrolling upward within it. "Liquidated all your assets seventy years ago," he read. "Stocks, bonds, real estate. Sold your haulage firms." He leaned to one side so he could see me around the infosheet. "Why?"

"That's none of your business."

"Yes." He chuckled. "I guess." He tapped the desk again and the infosheet vanished. Without its illumination, all kinds of shadows seemed to lean in from the edges of the room. "What do you do with all the money?"

"Count it."

He laughed, and for a moment I remembered the broad-shouldered athlete he had been. His laugh had always seemed larger than life. "Well," he said, "look at us."

"I recall we both made our own choices," I said. I sipped my drink again and settled a little further back into the big button-backed leather armchair.

"I wasn't expecting you for another couple of years," he said, picking up his glass and leaning forward in his chair.

"I didn't come here from Earth. My service forwarded your

message."

"Where were you?"

"Raul," I said, "why don't you just shine a bright light in my eyes, get Sheldon to work me over a bit, and *get to the point?*"

He laughed again. This time Sheldon joined in. Raul took another swallow of his drink. Suddenly he didn't seem quite so old and ill any more. He looked wise and capable and a bit scary. I sat where I was while they got over their hilarity.

"Well," Raul said finally to Sheldon, "let's show the man what we brought him all this way to see."

Sheldon reached into his jacket and took out a tapboard. He touched a couple of points and a huge infosheet came into being across the front of the room and drove the shadows back where they'd come from.

The sheet filled with a vista of flat green and brown marshland broken by big bare rocky hills that looked as if they had been dropped at random from orbit. I felt a cold sensation in the pit of my stomach, looking at that bleak landscape again.

"You'll recognise it, of course," said Raul. "That big rock over to the left is where we buried JJ. We turned the whole delta into a reserve for the rockers...oh, fifteen years ago, I guess. They were getting *endangered.* We had to do something."

"This is not funny," I told him.

He looked at me and tipped his head over to one side. The infosheet's illumination turned his face into an alien landscape of light and shadow. "No," he agreed finally. "No, I guess not. Cut to the rover, would you, Shel?"

Sheldon nodded and touched the tapboard again. The sheet cut dizzyingly to a lurching image of sedge and murky water.

"We sent a rover out from the ranger station about an hour ago," said Raul. "Thought you'd appreciate some live feed on this."

The image tilted up until we were looking out over the tough marsh grass towards one of the big rocky hills a few hundred metres away. There were large rounded objects scattered all over the hill.

The rover moved forward, highstepping to avoid tripping on half-submerged obstacles. As it neared the rock I could see that the rounded objects were big huts expertly woven from marsh grass. And they weren't scattered all over the rock. They were arranged in neat lines, with wide streets between them. I felt the back of my neck prickle.

"Started about ten years ago," Raul was saying. "At first we thought it was some new behaviour pattern, something we hadn't recorded before. Maybe something akin to the behaviour of weaver birds. We didn't know. We shot some really fine wildlife documentary footage, though. I expect you'll want to watch it later."

Little thready curls of smoke were rising from swan-necked chimneys woven into the roofs of the huts...

"Fire." Raul sighed. "Well, *that* took us *all* by surprise. That was about when I realised we might be in trouble. A year or so later, they were using writing."

Familiar six-legged shapes were moving in an orderly manner along the streets. Some of them seemed to have stopped to chat to each other. A few of them had paused to watch the rover clambering up the rocky slope out of the marsh. They were all wearing clothing.

"You'll remember the rockers, I guess," Raul said. "Real hard to catch, but good eating if you did manage to stop one of them. Made them real popular with hunters." He drained his glass and put it on the desk. "Which is our problem."

"This is crazy," I said, getting up and going over to the infosheet. "Rockers don't build houses and wear clothes." I turned to look at him. "They're animals."

He nodded. "That's what they were when we arrived. It's

not what they are now."

I looked at the sheet again, feeling sick. One of the rockers was approaching the rover, its right foreleg held high as if in greeting. Its feathery topknot waved in the breeze. It was wearing a well-tailored all-over garment which seemed to be composed of many pockets sewn together.

"We have, you'll be surprised to learn, no idea what is going on here," Raul said. "Although we have theories coming out of our ears. The one I like is that this is all actually a part of the species' life-cycle. They spend millions of years in various presentient stages and then they suddenly get smart in a hell of a hurry. Some of my guys think the change might have been triggered by predation pressure from us. I've got one guy – you'll meet him – thinks they might wind up smarter than us."

"This is crazy," I murmured again, shaking my head. The rocker had walked right up to the rover, close enough for me to see the square pupils of its eyes. Its big flappy lips were moving, though there was no audio feed to bring us any sounds it was making. "Is this thing *talking* to the rover?"

Raul chuckled. "Jesus, yes. They just love to talk. They'll drop what they're doing and natter for hours on end. Some of them speak pretty good English."

I covered my eyes with my hands.

"See why I asked you to come?" Raul said.

"Genocide," I said without taking my hands from my face.

"Any way you cut it," he agreed. "For around two hundred years we used the only other known intelligent species in the galaxy as a food animal. And made boots from their hides. Pretty good boots, too," he added, almost nostalgically.

I lowered my hands. "But they *weren't* intelligent."

Raul scowled and his whole face creased up like an old cider apple. "Hard to imagine the UNSA seeing it that way."

"Neil's right, Granddad," Sheldon chipped in with the tone

of voice of someone revisiting an old argument. "This is unprecedented. There's no way anyone could have predicted it."

I tried to think. "I suppose it's too much to hope for that the Agency don't know about this."

Raul rubbed a hand over his bare scalp. "Well," he admitted ruefully, "we did make an error or two, back in the early days."

I felt my heart sink. "What did you do?"

"We put out a press release," said Sheldon.

"You did *what?*"

Raul raised a hand for calm. "Back when this started we didn't know what the hell was going on," he said. "So we threw a fifty-kilometre exclusion zone around the rocker reservation while we tried to work out what to do, and to stop people wondering why we'd done it we put out a press release saying we were trying to protect the rockers from hunters."

I sighed. "And?"

"The Agency's got some intelligence officers here. I don't mind; it's just a fact of life, and we know who they all are anyway. A couple of them dressed up as hunters and went out into the Delta and tried to get into the reservation."

"They were arrested before they got anywhere near the rockers," said Sheldon. "We fined them for trying to enter a protected area." He chuckled. "And for hunting without a licence."

I looked from one to the other. "You boys should go into showbusiness," I told them.

"It's occurred to me," said Raul.

"So the Agency doesn't know the rockers have suddenly become intelligent. But it does know they've become endangered." I shook my head. "Do I have to guess what happens next?"

Raul shrugged. "I've been getting some scary emails from Earth asking about the rockers. Not directly from the Agency, from animal rights organisations, academics, concerned citizens, the UN Endangered Species Programme."

"Not hard to work out where they're really from, though," Sheldon put in.

"The way I see it, the Agency's going to try and use the rockers' endangered status to pry up the corners of the agreements JJ made with them," Raul said. "Give themselves a legal pretext for a presence on Reith."

"And when they actually go and see the rockers they're going to get the shock of their lives," I said.

"Any day now there'll be a carrier full of Marines and lawyers and xenobiologists and Christ only knows what else docking at Overlook, and shortly after that, my friend, you and I will be in all kinds of trouble." Raul drove his chair back to the bar and filled his glass.

"They want Reith."

"Of course they want Reith. They've always wanted Reith." He capped the vodka bottle and rotated his chair. "You know what Agency colonies are like."

"Can they do it?"

"What do *you* think, Neil? This bunch of wildcatters invaded Reith and proceeded to eat an intelligent species. You can imagine how *that'll* look."

"We stop being brave pioneers and become a bunch of clumsy amateur eco-unfriendly greedheads?"

He snorted. "We'll be lucky if they don't call for the death penalty."

That seemed a bit extreme, but I hadn't been on Earth for quite a while and the Agency had always been full of vindictive little clerks. I said, "Not that *you're* too worried about that."

I heard Sheldon take a sharp breath; clearly nobody spoke to the Planetary Commissioner like this, but Raul put his head back and laughed. "Well," he said, "we've got enough money to keep this thing in the courts for years, and it's true that I'll be long gone by the time there's a verdict, so in that respect I don't give a shit. But we've done something good here, Neil. I don't want that devalued."

"The place has been successful," I agreed. "I'm impressed."

Raul smiled and took a swig of whisky. "You haven't even seen the best bit yet. Shel?"

Sheldon fiddled with the tapboard and the rover started to move again, stepping confidently through the rocker village. Creatures which I had always associated with a good meal stepped out of the way to let the strange mechanical man pass. Some of them paused in their business and tried to engage the rover in conversation, then moved on when it was obvious that the machine didn't want to chat. I began to get the old itchy urge to run away.

The very crest of the hill was bare of dwellings, but it was crowned with a circle of standing stones that came up to the rover's waist. A couple of rockers were standing inside the circle, next to a big stone that sat at the highest point of the hill. They watched the rover incuriously as it stepped into the circle and began to walk around the central stone.

"They got religion about five years ago," said Raul. "Which is when I started trying to get in touch with you. This is a representation of their God."

As the rover moved, I saw that the central stone had been carved with a face about a metre across. At first it was just a nose poking out from around the edge of the stone. Then the lips came into view, and the hairline, then the eye sockets, the cheekbones. The rover stopped in front of the face.

I put my hand to my mouth, but a strangled little sound still made it past my palm.

"Personally," Raul said, "I think it's a pretty good likeness."

***

My bedroom was beautiful. Heavy velvet curtains over windows that opened onto a broad balcony. Blond oak-panelled walls. Pretty good Shaker-style furniture. A carpet with a pile you could lose a badger in. A double bed as soft as sleep and as deep as a French philosopher, covered with a duvet like a centrally-heated cloud and pillows that cradled your head like the first girl you ever kissed. After three years of the variable comforts of Push boats I should have slept like a baby.

I sat out on the balcony, on a porch swing that came complete with squeaky pivots, and sipped from a bottle of Glenmorangie that Raul had thoughtfully provided along with towels and a squeeze-bag of soap for the shower.

You travel light and you travel fast, and nothing can ever hurt you. That's the Law. One of the unbreakable constants of the Universe. Like the one that says you can't travel faster than the speed of light.

I sipped some more Scotch. The weather was mild enough for me to sit out here wearing my shorts and a teeshirt, even though it was almost one in the morning. Away down the valley, little twinkling lights among the trees marked the other houses on Raul's estate, and beyond them was a faint glow on the underside of the clouds that I presumed was where Jakobstown was.

I remembered when there were no people here, five years ago, or two hundred years ago. I remembered being strapped into a command couch in *Mason*'s control room and watching the planet scroll across the displays. I remembered thinking, "*Fuck, that looks nice, that'll do.*" I remembered John-Jakob bouncing from one side of the bridge to the other in great slow extravagant freefall cartwheels, gleefully shouting, "I want it! I want it! I want it!" I remembered everyone else laughing.

The system had already been mapped by fast-flyby probes,

but Reith's World – eventually just Reith – turned out to be a lot more habitable than the probe data had suggested. Its climate, except around the little polar icecaps, was agreeably temperate, its flora and fauna unthreatening and – with very few exceptions – delicious. The colony hit Reith like a virus to which the planet had no immunity and it was already spreading out across the world when I left two years later.

I held the bottle up to the weak light from Reith's natural moon. I'd managed to drink two-thirds of it and I still didn't feel remotely drunk or tired.

I had travelled for three years, and somewhere in the complex maths of the Push seventy years went by without me. And four months ago – or five years, depending on how good your Push motors are – Raul's message caught up with me. *We have a problem.*

Somewhere above me, in the great nest of chimneys that ran the length of the roof, a night-bird struck up a heartbreakingly beautiful song that sounded as if it was being played on a tiny steam calliope, and I cringed. The song stopped, then the bird made a noise, in a spookily deep and rasping voice, that sounded eerily like, "Yer grandma's dead! Yer grandma's dead! Yer grandma's dead!" before flapping off into the darkness. Of all Reith's flora and fauna, I had always hated grandmother birds the most.

I drew my arm back and pitched the bottle over the balcony rail as hard as I could. It sailed out into the night, turning end over end as it went. I sat listening for a long time, but I never heard it hit the ground.

Two

The problem with the Push is that if you use it often enough, you start to think you're immortal. When I first came to Reith, I could drink a bottle of Scotch, stay up half the night arguing with somebody, get involved in a medium-to-serious brawl, and still get up the next morning and perform a number of useful, if physically undemanding, tasks.

Now I was forty years old, I couldn't do those things any more, and it was almost two o'clock in the afternoon before I managed to haul my complaining body out of the bedroom and down the stairs.

"Good lord," Raul said when he saw me. "You've become a drunk."

"*You* can talk," I muttered.

"Yes, but I've had longer to practice," he said. He moved his chair back a metre or so to let me stagger to the bottom of the stairs. He shook his head. "That's really very sad."

"Raul," I managed to say, "do you have access to automated

medical facilities here?"

He looked down at himself, at the chair. "I dunno," he said. "What do *you* think?"

There was a state-of-the-art autodoc in a cupboard under the stairs. I stuck my arm into it and after five minutes I felt so good that I seriously considered standing there for the rest of my life.

"And you're telling me you don't have this sort of thing for *horses?*" I said. Clearly they didn't have anything that could fix the damage the fall had caused him, either.

Raul sucked his teeth noisily. "You know," he said, "if I'd known what was going to happen to us I might have tried to talk the rest of you out of it."

I shook my head. "JJ would never have let you."

"Personally," he said, "I think you would still have become a drunk."

All the readouts on the autodoc had turned green. I was well again. Unwillingly, I pulled my arm out and looked at it. The autodoc had tattooed the face of Wile E Coyote on my forearm. "That's *really* funny," I said.

Raul grinned. "A chap's got to get his laughs where he can find them. Do you feel well enough for breakfast?"

"I'm so hungry, I could eat a rocker. Hooves and all."

Raul stopped grinning. "I don't know why I ever thought you'd take this situation seriously."

"A chap's got to get his laughs where he can find them."

***

Breakfast was bacon, eggs, fried kidneys, baked beans, coffee, black pudding, fried potatoes, coffee, orange juice, toast, fried bread, grilled sausages and more coffee. And that was just what *I* ate. I drank another mug of coffee and wondered if there was any way to get Raul's autodoc out of its cupboard and take it with me everywhere.

Raul watched me eat with the bitter ennui of a man whose doctor has prescribed him a bowl of muesli for breakfast for the rest of his life. "What was it you used to call that?" he asked.

I looked up. "Beg pardon?"

He nodded at my plate, mopped clean with a butter-slathered wad of white bread. "That transport café breakfast you were always wolfing down back home."

I grinned. "'Cholesterol frenzy.'"

"Hm."

"Hey, don't blame me. You served it. All I did was eat it."

"I thought it would make you feel at home." He shook his head. "I never understood how someone with so much money could eat so much crap."

"It's not crap," I protested. "It contains a large number of the main food groups."

"Have you any idea what that stuff does to your arteries?"

I shrugged and finished my coffee. "I'll just stick my hand in your autodoc for a couple of hours."

"You are not going back into that cupboard."

I sat back in my chair. "Oh, am I not?"

"You are not." Raul steered his chair out from the other end of the table and rolled it forward until we were almost knee to knee. "I saw that look on your face when you were in there. You spend any more time with that thing and you're going to need a psychiatrist."

"What, you have an *auto*psychiatrist?" I asked, widening my eyes.

He shook his head in disgust. "Oh, fuck off."

"Love to." I poured out another mug of coffee. "Unfortunately…"

Raul drove the chair over to one of the floor-to-ceiling windows that let light flood into the breakfast room. It looked out onto an enormous sloping lawn that dropped down to a distant screen of trees, just as it had in his father's house back in Berkshire. He looked at the view for a while; it was anybody's guess what he saw when he looked out of these windows. Was he on Reith, or was he back home? I wondered which of us needed the psychiatrist.

Finally he said, "Have you had any ideas?"

"I thought I might sightsee for a while. Buy some souvenirs. Leave again."

Still looking out of the window, he said, "I dragged you all this way because I literally have no idea what to *do*, Neil. This situation is beyond me. I need some help."

I picked up my mug and got up and walked over to him. "I always liked this view," I said.

He glanced up at me, then back at the lawn beyond the window. "You know the house is still there? Back in Berkshire? I never sold it; my managers rent it out for corporate events. Media people, mostly. Conferences on the semiotics of advertising. I can't believe people are still having conferences about that stuff; you'd think they'd have figured it all out by now."

"It's just an excuse to get out of the office, get drunk and get laid," I told him. "That's all it ever was."

He scratched the back of his neck. "I know," he said sourly. "It just annoys me to think the house is being used as some kind of corporate brothel."

I drank some coffee. "Ever think of going back?"

Raul shook his head. "Nah. You?"

"I wasn't wild about the place when we got back from Pictoris. Didn't like the movies."

"So, what. You're just going to keep wandering about?"

I went back to the long sideboard, on the top of which were arrayed the silver trays from which I had looted my belated breakfast. I picked up a crispy slice of bacon which I'd missed, and I carried it back to the windows. I bit off a piece.

"I never begged anyone for anything before, Neil," Raul said. "Never in my life. My hand to God."

"I know," I said. I put my hand on his shoulder; his skin, through the grey cotton robe he was wearing, was feverishly hot. "I know, Raul. And you're not begging now."

"So you'll help us?"

The idea of the Agency taking over on Reith really hurt. I said, "You said you had some people working on the problem already. I should probably speak with them. Look at the recordings you talked about."

He looked at me. "And go to the reservation."

I thought about what he had shown me last night, popped the rest of the bacon into my mouth, and muttered, "Well..."

"Oh, come on, Neil," he said. "Don't tell me you're not *curious.*"

"I can be out of here on the next boat," I said. "The pilot who brought me in will still be at Overlook; he's probably still for hire. I can be *light years* from here before anything happens, and my money's so well hidden you'd need a psychic to find it."

"We can't rule out the possibility that the Agency has psychics," Raul told the view morosely. "But point taken. You have nothing to lose. Congratulations. Well done. Are you going to tell me that you told me so?"

"No." Although I *had* told him so. I had warned everybody that the Agency would come back into our lives in some exotic and unthinkable way, and nobody had listened, but I didn't feel any great joy in being proved right.

There was a knock on the door, and Mrs Tring, Raul's housekeeper, poked her head into the room. "Someone to see you, Mr Marquez."

Raul turned his chair from the windows. "Of course, Mrs Tring; I'd almost forgotten. Show her in, please." Mrs Tring returned to the hallway and Raul looked at me. "I took the liberty of asking one of our rocker experts to pop round to meet with you. I hope you don't mind."

I said, "If it…" and the words just trailed off in my mouth as Laura walked into the room.

She was wearing a pair of jeans and a yellow sweatshirt and her hair was bound into a yard-long plait that dangled down her back and she was carrying a small briefcase and apart from the clothes she looked more or less the way she had that evening at John-Jakob's penthouse suite in Warsaw when I had first met her. I made a number of discreet prelingual noises.

She came across the room and ignored me completely, which was also what had happened that night in Warsaw. She bent and kissed Raul on both cheeks and said, "Hi, Granddad," and that broke the spell. "Introduce me to your friend?"

Raul had an evil grin on his face. "Neil Hanson, Susan-Lianne Vaughan. Susan-Lianne –"

She put out her hand and grinned perkily at me. "Suli."

We shook hands. "Neil." I wanted to go back to the autodoc for a while.

"Granddad Raul says you've come to help us with our problem."

I said "Um," and mentally congratulated myself for being able to say that much.

She looked solemn and I felt my heart break. "It's a big problem. We need all the help we can get."

I said, "Aha."

She looked at Raul. "Is he all right?" she asked.

"He's come a long way," Raul told her.

"I was thinking we could go for a picnic," she said to him. "Get to know each other. Talk about things."

Raul's expression brightened. "I think that's a great idea, Suli. What do you think about that, Neil?"

I couldn't stop looking at her. I managed to say, "Hm?"

"Suli wants to take you for a picnic, Neil," Raul said. "You think you could manage a picnic?"

I finally let go of Suli's hand. "I think I need to talk to…um…Granddad Raul in private for a couple of minutes," I said to her. "Would you excuse us?"

She didn't look offended, or even particularly surprised. Raul had probably told her that this was the way I normally behaved. She just sort of *twinkled* at me, then kissed Raul again and left the breakfast room and closed the door behind her, and when the door was closed I leaned down and grabbed the front of Raul's robe.

"You bastard," I said. "What did you do, *clone* her?"

Raul smiled and shook his head. "She's Laura's great-granddaughter."

"You're kidding."

He shook his head again. "Amazing, really. Laura's kids and grandkids didn't look anything like her."

"It's a cheap trick, and I'm not going to fall for it," I told him.

He put on an expression of innocent surprise. "What?"

"You know what I'm talking about."

"Neil." He looked hurt. "I'm hurt. Suli knows more about the rockers than practically anybody else on Reith. If we're going to sort out this mess somehow, we're going to need her help."

I felt as though my hangover was coming back; I wanted to go back to the cupboard under the stairs. "Did JJ have any children? Are you going to spring some handsome wankers on me?" And then an appalling thought occurred to me. "Did *I* have any children?"

"John-Jakob had a chromosomal abnormality that all the money on Earth couldn't fix. He couldn't have children without zygote screening, and we weren't set up to do that." He looked momentarily angry. "He left behind a lot of miscarriages, stupid bastard." He blinked up at me. "You, on the other hand, have a *lot* of descendants on Reith." He smiled. "Would you like to meet them?"

I let him go and backed away. "No."

"I kept track of them, down the years. Quite a lot of them are nice people. Some of them are doing useful jobs."

"You've grown up to be a *really* nasty old man."

He spread his hands. "My opinion? If you don't want descendants, you shouldn't have sex with every admiring colonist who comes along. Did I mention that to you at the time? It's all such a long time ago, I don't remember."

"You know very well that you mentioned it to me, you bastard."

He shrugged. "Yes, well, I knew it was pointless. You were already on your fifth divorce when we first met."

"Fourth," I said. "*Fourth* divorce."

"You know," he said conversationally, "a disinterested observer might look at your marital record and conclude that either you were really bad at choosing partners, or you were just impossible to live with."

"Fuck you." I went back to the windows.

"You've got to make a choice, Neil," Raul said.

"That's good, coming from you. You never made a choice in your life."

There was a silence from the other side of the room. Then Raul said, "That's not fair."

I turned to look at him. "You brought me here to decide what you should do. You just let yourself be bullied into every decision you ever made. And the rest of the time you just hummed and hahed and let other people decide for you."

He gave me his scary and wise look, and it was just as scary and wise in daylight as it had been last night. "I decided to stay here with these people," he said evenly.

That stopped me short. I scowled. "I'm sorry, Raul."

"You'd better be, you son of a bitch."

I turned from the windows and looked at him.

"Oh, go and have a picnic," he said irritably. "Pretty young girl, nice lunch, beautiful scenery. How can it hurt?"

"Your memory's not as good as it used to be," I told him. "Otherwise you'd know just how much it can hurt."

***

Suli was waiting for me in the hallway. "And?" she asked as I went past.

"And what?"

She fell into step beside me and we went out through the front door and down the cinder path towards the gravelled driveway of the house. "And do you want a picnic?"

"Yes, let's assume I want a picnic," I said. I stopped on the driveway and looked around. "Where's your car?" I looked at her. "What are you laughing at?"

***

On a tree-screened landing pad on the other side of Raul's estate, Suli had an aircraft which looked like a two-person moth and flew at Mach 3. She grinned at me as I strapped myself into the copilot's seat. "You're not afraid of flying, are you?" she teased.

"Let's just pretend I am and fly accordingly," I told her, and she laughed.

We flew down the coast a couple of hundred kilometres, to a great area of chalk downland which I was relieved to see had not yet been developed. Suli landed us at a little airport, grabbed a wicker picnic hamper from a storage locker on the jet, and drove us the rest of the way in an electric buggy about the size of a computer printer.

It was a nice day, warm but pleasantly breezy, and there was a path of compacted chalk which gave the buggy a smooth ride. She drove us another few kilometres and all we did was exchange small talk. Finally we stopped at a picnic spot on the great curling brow of a hill, and while she took her basket from the buggy's luggage compartment I looked out into the enormous green rolling misty distances. I could see all the way to the coast, and a sea that looked as if it had been waiting for several million years for Winslow Homer to come along and paint it. I remembered when there were no picnic facilities here. Or chalk paths. Or airports. Or people.

I heard her calling my name. I turned and saw that she had opened the hamper and spread a white tablecloth on the grass, on which she was now arranging a number of white containers. I walked over.

"I didn't know what you'd like to eat," she told me. "So I got a bit of everything."

The white containers were cardboard boxes from a deli in Jakobstown. Poppy-seeded knot rolls, pastries, various patés, crackers, crusty baguettes, really *excellent* butter, some cheeses that were even better, an assorted fruit platter, a carafe of what turned out to be a snappy little white wine, a thermos of coffee.

I sat down beside her. "I don't know how much help I can be," I said.

She poured a glass of wine and handed it to me. "This must be really disorientating for you."

"It's a first," I admitted.

"I never met my great-grandmother," she told me. "Go on, eat. I brought it all this way."

"You missed an experience, not meeting Laura."

"Granddad Raul says that, too."

I looked at her. "Why do you call him *Granddad?* You're not related, are you?"

"No, but he's always sort of kept an eye on us – me and my family. He's sort of my honorary granddad."

"Hmm." I wondered if any of *my* descendants called Raul 'Granddad.'

"He asked you to come, and here you are," she said.

"And here I am," I agreed, sorting through the food and electing to smear some paté on a cracker. "I cannot argue with you there. I am certainly here."

"That has to count for something."

I ate the cracker. It was, by some considerable distance, the most exquisite thing I had ever tasted. I sat there for a moment, utterly baffled. Then I trowelled paté onto another cracker and ate that too. Then I ate another one. At some point I realised that Suli was frowning at me. "Beg pardon?" I said.

"How long has it been since you last had a good meal?" she asked.

"Breakfast was pretty outstanding," I admitted, anointing another cracker. "Before that?" I tried to remember the last really memorable meal I'd had. "Your grandparents probably still hadn't been born yet." I ate the cracker and started to prepare another one. I wondered distantly whether every experience on Reith had become addictive, or if it was just me. "Can I get this stuff in industrial quantities?" I asked.

Suli got to her feet and looked down at me. "It's a long way to come, for someone who says he's in trouble. I don't think I know more than two or three people who would do that for *anybody.*"

I ate the cracker and it was just as good as all the other ones. I thought I could haul this stuff around the galaxy and make a fortune. "Well, I wouldn't do it for just *anybody…*"

She nodded. "I've talked with Granddad Raul about it, but

it's not the same. He's..."

"Old," I said.

She nodded again. "I don't know why it should make such a difference." She asked, "How old are you?"

"I'm forty."

She sighed. "You're four hundred and seventy-seven. I looked it up. And Granddad Raul's four hundred and sixty."

"He hasn't worn as well as me."

She frowned at me again, and for a moment I saw Laura frowning at me. "It makes you uncomfortable, doesn't it? Being a hero."

"Suli," I said as seriously as I could, "none of us were heroes. We were young and bored and lonely and we had much too much money. It just seemed like a good idea at the time."

She laughed. "The history books don't put it quite like that."

"They won't. 'Seemed like a good idea at the time' doesn't exactly make big news, historically speaking."

"I'm going out to the Reserve tomorrow. Will you come with me?"

I lay back on the grass and clasped my hands behind my head and watched the clouds ambling across the sky.

I heard her sigh again. She slurped some wine. "How was it, then?"

"How was what?"

"If the history books are wrong, what was it really like?"

I watched the clouds for a while longer, thinking about this. She must have thought I wasn't going to answer, because she turned and walked to the brow of the hill and put her hands in her pockets and stood looking out across the downs.

"The only thing we really had in common was John-Jakob's Big Idea," I said finally.

She didn't turn round.

"We were all part of the same social circle," I told the

clouds. "Me, Raul, John-Jakob, Laura. We'd all lost our parents and we were all very very wealthy. I mean, *beyond* wealthy. We were some of the richest people on Earth. And we were bored." I paused a moment, thinking. "Actually, that's not fair. I can't speak for the others. But I was just bobbing along on a fluffy pink cloud of wealth. My parents died in a plane crash; my brother and I hadn't spoken to each other in ten years. I was bored, everything was too *safe*. The most interesting thing I did was play tennis with Raul. His parents had just died as well, and he knew John-Jakob, who had been shepherding the Reith billions for five or six years, and John-Jakob knew Laura, and we all just sort of drifted together."

She still didn't turn round.

"The Push was still pretty much in its infancy back then," I went on. "The earliest Push motors went into production when I was fifteen or sixteen. There was a lot of excitement. Faster-than-light technology. Wow. The stars were ours. Except the time dilation effect was something *outrageous*. I can't remember exactly, but it was something like five hundred to one. You could get to Proxima Centauri and back in about five years, but when you got home you'd find that two and a half thousand years had passed. It was a white elephant."

That made her turn round. "Sorry? It was a what?" She giggled.

"A white elephant."

She shook her head. "I never heard that one before."

I wondered if I was the only living human being who used that phrase any more. "Anyway. Research-And-Development never stands still. By the time I met John-Jakob, Push motors were a lot more efficient and the time dilation was way down. It was low enough to use inside the Solar System, and there was an unmanned UNSA probe on its way to Proxima Centauri.

"John-Jakob had this idea that there was no real reason not

to use insystem Push boats for an extrasolar trip, so long as you didn't care about the time dilation. He said the only thing that stopped people actually going off to the stars was that everybody they knew would have been dead for a couple of hundred years when they got back. He said everybody just presumed that colonists would want to come back at some point."

Suli came back and stood over me. "It's that simple? You just didn't care?"

"I told you; we didn't have anything to keep us on Earth. We didn't have anyone we would have missed." I sat up and picked up my glass. "We did have a couple of very long nights at Raul's house in Berkshire, discussing it." I drank some wine and picked up a pastry. "As I remember, the thing we were most worried about was technology catching up with us. We could have set out, spent a hundred years or so in the Push, and got to the other end, only to find a bunch of people waiting for us who had got there with more efficient motors."

"What would you have done if that had happened?"

"Personally, I would have blushed somewhat."

What we decided in the end was that, for our purposes, it was a worthwhile risk. John-Jakob wanted to load the odds in our favour and buy heavily into Push research in order to slow it down, but Laura managed to persuade him that this smacked a little too much of industrial espionage, and I convinced him by pointing out that it might not even work. It was a close-run thing, though; once John-Jakob got an idea into his head it tended to stay there until he got what he wanted. That's another thing the history books don't tell you.

We packed up the picnic things and got on the little electric cart and headed back to the airport.

"We picked up two old insystem colony boats that were going to be scrapped," I told her as she drove. "*Mason* and *Dixon*, bless them. They weren't much more than hollowed-out asteroids slung between big inefficient Push motors. Then we negotiated a nominal fee and a percentage with a bunch of freefall miners out in the Belt who wanted to try mining the rubble halo around Beta Pictoris. Two years there, a year hanging about until they established themselves, and two years back. When we got home, the miners had been making money for us for about a hundred years."

"What did you do for the four years you were in transit?" she asked. "They didn't have suspension back then, did they?"

Well, I couldn't fault her research. "None of us had ever met a freefall miner until we started advertising for the trip. They spend all their time out in space in ships not much bigger than your aeroplane. Months and months on their own, going from rock to rock looking for valuable minerals. If you stick a lot of them together in a confined space, they start getting cranky. *Mason* and *Dixon* weren't small boats, but we spent a lot of the outbound leg breaking up fights and keeping the peace between various groups." Actually, by the time we arrived at Beta Pic we had half the miners locked up in their quarters. There had been assassinations, peace treaties, executions, marriages of convenience, apocalyptic cults and two messiahs. We unloaded the miners and their ships and their bubble habitats and I was all for turning around and going home right away, but JJ said we had to wait until they were capable of supporting themselves. I never wanted to see another freefall miner again.

"Commander Reith was right," she said.

"Beg pardon?"

"About the miners. You couldn't just turn tail and abandon them."

"It would not have been an effort," I assured her. I didn't add that the experience of being told that JJ was right about something had grown old for me more than a century ago.

"You were responsible for them."

"We were contracted to haul them out to Beta Pic, not to babysit them, Suli. Suppose we'd been hauling a boatload of chickens. Would we have been responsible for all of them after we delivered them?"

"They weren't chickens," she said. "They were people."

I watched the landscape roll by. "Well, *miners*, anyway…"

She glanced thoughtfully at me, and we drove for quite a while in silence.

Finally, she asked, "What about on the way back?"

The way back? Oh, a dream of drifting weightless through caverns measureless to Man, great echoing empty chambers, the sound of the great centrifuges which gave a semblance of gravity to the living quarters, that peculiar almost-not-there vibration of the old generation Push motors carrying us home…

"It wasn't much different from being on Earth, really," I said. "With the miners gone, there was a *lot* of room. We didn't see each other for days on end. Raul and I played tennis in zero-gee. I taught myself to play the bassoon."

Suli laughed. "The what?"

"Big woodwind instrument." I saw the look on her face. "You blow into it. It's kind of…" I sketched the bassoon's curves and straight lines in the air, saw it wasn't making any sense to her. "Look it up."

She laughed. "You spent two years learning how to play an instrument?"

"I didn't take an instruction manual. When I took the damn thing on board I didn't even know which bit you blew into; I had to learn it from scratch." I was actually quite proud of that. I'd got pretty good. "We all did different things. Your great-grandmother wrote a novel."

"I know. *Diddums Looks At The Sky From Different Places On Earth.* I've got a signed copy."

So did I. It was in my bag back at Raul's house. "They

turned it into a really shitty film."

"So all you did for two years was play tennis and write novels and learn to play the baboon?"

"*Bass*oon. We played a lot of paintball as well." I shrugged and watched the scenary go by.

She laughed again. And she shook her head. And she laughed some more. And every now and then while she flew us back to Jakobstown something seemed to occur to her, and she laughed some more.

***

"It's a nice story," she said later. "But it doesn't really have an ending, does it?"

"That's what happens in the real world," I told her. "Stories just go on and on."

We were sitting in a restaurant on Jakobstown's West Side, down by the river. Lots of tables in a dimly-candlelit room. On the plate in front of me a small four-legged crab lay on its back, its insides opened to the world. At last I'd managed to encounter something on Reith that I couldn't eat. Even drenched in melted garlic butter the thing tasted like the bottom of a pond. Suli seemed to like them, though; she was on her second.

"That's not what I mean," she said.

"No, I know." I looked down at the crab, pushed it to one side, and started to fork through my side-salad. "It's just not a very interesting story, Suli. Young rich people go flying about the Galaxy. Yawn."

"*I'm* interested."

"No you're not. You heard this story from Raul already. All you want to do is lull me into a state of warm happiness and then get me to agree to go out to the Reservation with you tomorrow and talk me into helping you."

Give her credit; she didn't deny it. "Will you go?"

I put some salad in my mouth and chewed. Some imbecile had dressed it with parmesan, which to my mind was *not* the way civilised people treated salad. I put my fork down. "Is *any* of the food in this place edible?" I asked, loud enough for all the waiters and most of the other diners to hear.

She looked down at the crab on her plate. "These are delicacies."

"Not where *I* come from, they're not."

"Okay." She sat back and picked up her wineglass. "What are the delicacies where *you* come from?"

"I'm from London; we didn't have a native cuisine." I thought about pie and mash and jellied eels, and I shook my head. "Steak and kidney pie. Chicken tikka masala. A really *really* solid doner kebab – lots of shaved lamb and shredded lettuce and onions and tomatoes in a warm pitta bread. Fish and chips." I sat back too. Jesus, I hadn't tasted fish and chips for almost three hundred years. I looked at the ceiling, thinking about all the other things I hadn't tasted for a long time. "Pizza. You'd think pizza would travel, wouldn't you? Haven't seen a pizza since we came back from Pictoris. Sausage rolls."

"I beg your pardon?"

"Flaky pastry wrapped around a roll of sausage meat." I sketched it in the air, but I could see it was making no more impression than my description of a bassoon. "Jesus, I could make a fortune introducing sausage rolls and kebabs and pizza to this place."

"You think they'd sell here?"

"Suli, *all* right-thinking people like sausage rolls and kebabs and fish and chips. They're signs of a mature civilisation."

She laughed and drank some wine, but I was actually half-thinking about franchises.

***

When we got back from Pictoris, we found that things had changed, but not as much as we might have expected. Everyone we had known was dead, but we'd known that was going to happen. Fashions were different, the music scene was pretty strange, there were a few new countries and some of the old ones were gone. There had been a couple of wars, one of them nuclear in a limited way, and out of the aftermath of that the UN had somehow emerged as a global superpower, which was pretty freaky. There was an awful lot of porn in mainstream movies. Our money was still there, though, which made fitting back in fairly painless.

Research, of course, had not stood still while we were gone. A company in Seattle had perfected a way of putting people and animals into hibernation, which meant I would never have to share another long trip with a bunch of conscious freefall miners. And someone in Bonn had managed to work out a way of using quantum entanglement to build a device which transmitted information instantaneously to any point in the universe, no matter how far away it was, as long as one half of a pair of entangled atoms was there. This obviously imposed some limitations – you had to get that atom there in the first place – but eventually an informal trade grew up with Push boat pilots carrying entanglement lattices from colony to colony along with their regular cargo. Bandwidth was always a problem and in the early days the best anyone could do was send text messages and still images.

With the money from the Pictoris gig we retrofitted the boats with more efficient motors and got a contract with the UN Space Agency for a one-shot round-trip resupply to one of their colonies, a god-awful planet called New Hope whose atmosphere seemed to be mostly photochemical smog. We did moderately well out of that one, but when we returned to Earth our joint venture was two hundred years old, Beta Pictoris was surrounded by a halo of multimillionaire miners and we were rich beyond the dreams of avarice.

We had all been rich when John-Jakob first had the Big Idea. Now we were wealthier than some nations, but after a couple of months kicking our heels and trying to get used to Earth again, John-Jakob started to get itchy feet.

He wanted to buy some of the most up-to-date data available from the Agency's mapping programme and go out and found his own colony. Mining, manufacturing, medical research, everything would belong to us, lock, stock and barrel. Reith's World, he called it. Ego Trip, I called it.

He persuaded Laura first. Then he talked Raul into fronting up some of his money. Then one night in Bratislava we all went out and got drunk and the three of them talked me round.

We found a likely-looking prospect, filed a title for the planet, advertised for people who wanted to be colonists, fitted *Mason* and *Dixon* out with suspension equipment, and we schlepped thirty-two thousand paying passengers and a build-it-yourself colony to a new life among the stars. You can't do that any more. The Agency found a way to put a stop to it, eventually. Too many outfits were following our example and founding their own private planets. The Agency hates private enterprise.

***

At any one time, only about half a dozen people even have the vaguest idea of how the Push works.

I know this because I asked. None of my comrades ever showed the slightest interest in the technology in which we were entrusting our lives and our fortunes, so I thought one of us ought to find someone who could explain it to us.

I finally tracked down a professor of theoretical physics at the University of Chicago who was willing to talk, a whip-thin, haunted-looking bloke wearing a worn-out Packers sweatshirt. The first thing he said to me was, "At any one time, only about half a dozen people even have the vaguest idea of how the Push works," and for the next three hours I didn't understand a single word he said. It was like the whole middle of the day had been cut out and the ends butt-spliced together, because the next thing I remember is him sighing and saying, "You want to get a beer?" and two days later I woke up with a hangover in a commune in Kenosha and I was married to a girl named Congreave Mather, who was a member of a militant Leninist *parkour* troupe and claimed a direct line of descent from one of the Pilgrim Fathers, and after that I decided that the more arcane workings of the universe were best left to the half-dozen or so people in worn-out sweatshirts who claimed to understand them.

Anyway, despite being one of the most complex modes of transportation created by Man, Push boats were so simple to operate that you could train a bright six-year-old to pilot one in an afternoon. All you did was feed into the computer the coordinates for Point A and Point B – the place you were, and the place you wanted to go to – and then you went into suspension and waited to be thawed out in time to deal with any course corrections and tricky orbital insertions at the other end. Any emergencies en route that were serious enough for the boat to wake you up were probably not survivable anyway, and it took so long to become a functional human being again after a spell in suspension that by the time you were compos mentis the disaster would be long in the past. Probably better to just die in your sleep.

Having said that, we only had two boats, and it would have been handy for the colony to have both of them in case of disaster rather than letting me run off with one, so Raul piloted me to the Dependencies in *Mason*, dropped me off, and took the boat back to Reith alone. I joked that he was the most expensive chauffeur I'd ever had, but he didn't laugh. Because there were two of us, we did the flight in four-week shifts, one of us awake at all times, and during the handovers when we were both awake Raul never once tried to talk me into turning around and going back. The outbound leg took us a little over nine months, which with *Mason*'s old Push motors added up to a couple of weeks shy of a century in the real universe. We hung around in the Dependencies for a year or so, buying supplies for Raul to take back to Reith. We got *Mason*'s motors upgraded, which meant that when Raul finally went back it took him five months to get to Reith and only forty years passed outside the Push.

When Raul had finally made a decision, he had made the right one, and it had been a big one. He had decided to grow old and die with the people we brought to Reith. Actually, considering that the round-trip to the Dependencies lasted a hundred and forty-odd years, what he really decided to do was grow old and die with the *descendants* of the people we brought to Reith, but I suspected that Raul didn't make that distinction. He dropped me off and he turned round and went back, and that was what mattered.

So I supposed I owed him at least my undivided attention, and any advice I could come up with, whatever *that* was worth. Beyond that, I wasn't sure.

I sat up in bed and told the lights to come up to half brightness. I mashed the pillows down behind my back and told the house computer to search for Suli's phone number and dial it, and a few moments later a sleepy voice spoke from the empty air a few inches from my right ear.

"Mm, yeah?"

"I'll see you at the airport at seven o'clock tomorrow," I said.

There was a pause, then the voice said, "What, *morning?*"
Kids today.
I hung up.

Three

Sheldon drove me out to the airport in a ground vehicle that looked as if it had a Hummer and a Porsche Spyder not too far back in its ancestry.

"This is a really serious situation, Neil," he said when he had left Raul's estate and were driving down a smooth nano-fabricated highway of black stone towards Jakobstown.

"*You*," I told him, "can call me 'Mr Hanson.'"

"This is a really serious situation, *Mr Hanson*."

I rubbed my eyes. I should have told Suli to meet me at some civilised hour. Nine o'clock in the evening, maybe.

"I'm not a morning person," I said.

Sheldon glanced at me. "Was that an *apology*?"

I said, "I'm getting a little tired of everyone telling me how *serious* this situation is, Sheldon. I'm not stupid. I *know* how serious it is."

He shrugged. "I guess we're all worried you'll just take off."

Considering my past record regarding Reith, I supposed it was fair enough comment. "I can't understand what everybody thinks I can *do*," I said. "You *must* have people here who are brighter than me."

"Oh, absolutely," Sheldon said, a little more readily than I would have liked. "Although Grandfather's been trying to restrict it to Need To Know."

"Sheldon," I told him, "I am utterly baffled."

"Grandfather thinks a lot of you," he said. "You and he are the last of the...well, you know. You're his oldest friend. He needed help, he called you."

"You don't think so much of me, though," I said. "Do you."

He concentrated on driving for a while. Then he said, "Everyone learns about you guys at school. Grandfather, you, Commander Reith, Laura Marchmont. I don't think you realise how much you're part of our culture. Grandfather's..." he shook his head wonderingly. "Sometimes I think most of the population look on him as a kind of living legend. Like the Wizard of Oz or something. And then suddenly here *you* are."

"And I'm a disappointment."

"You're not what we learned about in school, *Mr Hanson.*"

"I never asked to be a hero," I said. "No one ever emailed me and asked my opinion. You can't blame me for that. All I was doing was making money."

He shook his head. "I mean, feet of clay and all that..."

"Fuck you, Sheldon."

"Fuck you too, *Mr Hanson.*"

Boy, that hero worship stuff really has a short half-life. "Would you have been happier if I'd just stayed in the history books?"

"Actually, yes."

"Fuck you, Sheldon."

"Fuck you too, *Mr Hanson.*"

"Okay, you can call me Neil if you want."

"Okay."

I looked at him. "Sheldon, what in Christ's name are you so *angry* about this morning?"

"*Are* you going to run away again?"

"Not just yet, no."

"If you abandon Grandfather again I'm going to come and find you."

I stared. "Sheldon," I said, not without some admiration, "are you *threatening* me?"

He concentrated on the road.

"Because if you're threatening me," I went on for a bit of fun, "you'd better mean it."

We drove in silence for a couple of klicks. I thought maybe I'd underestimated Sheldon, but I'd done that with lots of people in the past and there was no evidence that I was ever going to stop doing it.

"He's afraid," he said eventually.

"I beg your pardon?"

"He's afraid. What you did here, you and Grandfather and Commander Reith and Laura Marchmont…" He waved a hand in the air. "Well, just *look* at it."

"I've seen it, Sheldon. I'm proud of your ancestors, they did a great job." Although it might not have been quite so great if we hadn't brought a lot of nanoassemblers with us, programmed to produce everything from simple foods to tools to buildings. I honestly thought the colonists we had brought here were special people, but we had arrived with every technological advantage known to Man. If we'd just dropped them onto the planet with a bunch of hand-tools and some hogs they might not have done quite so well.

"It means a lot to Grandfather," said Sheldon. "*You* mean a lot to him."

"Look," I said, "I went through all this in my head last night. I owe Raul a big favour. Maybe more than one big favour. I'll do my best."

He glanced across at me with a look which told me that he thought my best might not be good enough.

"Oh, shut up and drive," I said, leaning back against the seat's head-rest. "I don't want to miss my flight."

***

Suli and her little jet were waiting for us in a discreet corner of the airport, well away from the prying eyes of ordinary travellers. She and Sheldon greeted each other with hugs that were a little too warm to be just friendship, and Sheldon left, but not before giving me what he probably thought was a scary stare. I made myself a mental note to tell him that I'd been given scary stares by professionals, and waved him goodbye.

"You have a problem with Sheldon?" Suli asked as we watched him drive away.

"Might do," I said absently. "Too soon to tell."

She was quiet a moment, then she said, "So, here you are."

"Let's not start that again," I told her, climbing up the short ladder into the belly of the aircraft. I heard her laugh as she followed me.

Inside, we strapped in to the cramped flight couches and Suli started to do the jet's preflight checks. I sat with my hands folded in my lap, staring out of the forward windows and wondering why I hadn't had the presence of mind to ignore Raul's emails.

I said, "Before we get there, is there anything I need to know?"

She looked at me. "Didn't you read the go-to I sent you?"

After I phoned her, Suli had emailed me a four hundred and seventy-two-page briefing document, with about fifteen hundred gigabytes of full-motion video, about the rockers. I had been tempted to throw it away and just wing it, but I had sat up for the rest of the night reading, skimming all the words of more than three syllables. Around four o'clock in the morning, gritty-eyed and achy, I had gone downstairs to see if the autodoc had anything which could help me, only to find that Raul had reprogrammed the thing to deny me access. Which I thought was a bit irresponsible. I mean, suppose I was seriously injured and needed the 'doc in a hurry?

I said, "I read the go-to. Is there anything I *need* to know?"

She sighed. "Their society isn't really hierarchical as such but, if it was, the guy we're going to see would be their headman."

"Rocker," I said.

"Beg pardon?"

"Rocker. Head rocker."

She looked across at me and frowned. Then she went back to the preflight checks. "Anyway, a couple of years ago the rockers started taking English names because we couldn't pronounce theirs. The head *rocker* calls himself Ringo. He's really, really bright."

I closed my eyes and put my head back against the headrest. "Don't tell me. They're all big fans of The Beatles."

Suli laughed and I opened my eyes and looked at her. "It's a bit more involved than that," she said, and I heard the turbines start to whine up to speed. "We were having some trouble trying to explain fiction to them; all the stories they tell are *true* stories, tribal stories, clan stories, old bits of race memory. They've got no idea that you can just make that kind of thing up for the purposes of entertainment." She flicked a couple of switches and said, "Jakobstown Control, this is RM239 requesting clearance for takeoff." She listened for a moment. "Thank you, Control. Anyway, a couple of us got this idea to just *show* them how entertainment works, so we got some entertainment decks and a bunch of old movies and took them out to Rockertown and we had a film show."

"Good grief," I said, trying to imagine a cinema full of rockers.

"Mm. Well, it kind of worked and it kind of didn't. Most of the younger ones sort of got the idea, but it just went by a lot of the older ones. They love Westerns, we found that out. They adored *Stagecoach*."

Oh, right. "The Ringo Kid."

"Not the original John Ford version, though. The remake, the one with Bing Crosby as Doc and Alex Cord as Ringo. The rockers can't stand black and white movies."

I looked out through the windscreen. "My head hurts," I said.

"Yeah?" She pushed a button on the control panel. "You wait until I introduce you to Ripley and Don Vito."

The jet gave a great squeal and jumped straight up into the sky.

***

The rocker reservation was about a hundred and fifty klicks west of Jakobstown, a huge area of marshes and braided river deltas into which some past ice age's glaciers had dropped enormous boulders. It was a landscape of sedge and brackish water broken by the hump-backs of great *kopjes* and it wasn't much use for anything – apart from the largest group of rockers on the planet – so JJ had decided to put Jakobstown's nuclear reactor there. The colony's assemblers could churn out outlandish quantities of room-temperature superconductor cable, at a fraction of a cent per hundred kilometres. We could have put the station halfway around the planet – hell, we could have put it in *orbit* – but JJ had said this was where it should be, and this was where it had been put.

Fusion power was cheap and clean. Unfortunately, the equipment to produce it was expensive, tricky to put together, bulky to haul, and needed trained personnel to maintain it. On the other hand, nuclear power was just cheap brute-force technology, Reith had an abundance of the requisite materials, and any idiot could run it. We meant to hit Reith aggressively, no messing about. Jakobstown needed electricity in large quantities and we couldn't run it off the dropships' power plants for ever, so we'd decided early on in the planning stages to build one nuclear reactor and then decommission it and drop the byproducts in Reith's sun when the colony became sophisticated enough to support fusion. We flew over it on the way in to Rockertown, still running, still nightmarishly racking up radioactivity.

"Hasn't anybody got rid of that thing yet?" I grumped as the streaked concrete of the complex passed beneath us.

"It's cheaper to keep it going," Suli said. "Have you any idea how much it costs to decommission a nuclear power station?"

"I'll write you a cheque," I told her and she laughed, but I wasn't kidding. "Could it have been the radiation?"

"Beg pardon?"

"The rockers suddenly getting clever. Could it have been radiation from the power station?"

"Oh." She shook her head. "No. It happened to rockers all over the planet, not just the ones living around here. We did genetic comparisons and there haven't been any mutations. As far as we can tell, the rockers now are just the same as the rockers were when you first landed here."

"Except...not."

"Except not," she said soberly. "Yes."

I watched out of the window as we banked over the power station. It would have been even easier to build a plant burning fossil fuels, but Laura had balked at that because of the emissions.

And besides, we weren't set up for the large-scale coal-mining or oil drilling and refining operation it would have needed to fuel a fossil station. Nuclear was quick and easy and we brought our own radioactives in a heavily-shielded pod that we attached to *Dixon*'s surface and then popped off and aerobraked into the atmosphere when we arrived. I rubbed my eyes. The Agency was right: we'd been amateurs, treating the galaxy like a big sparkly toy, raining death and pollution down on everywhere we went.

"What are you thinking about?" Suli asked.

I took my hand away from my eyes. "Happy thoughts," I told her. "I'm thinking nothing but happy thoughts."

***

"You know," Suli said, "if it bothered you this much, we could just have stuck your face into Grandpa Raul's autodoc and given you some cosmetic mods." We were standing beside the jet, which Suli had landed on a concrete pad beside the clutch of prefab buildings a couple of kilometres from Rockertown which comprised the rocker research institute, or whatever people here called it.

"Mm," I said. I was wearing a big pair of sunglasses and a baseball cap adorned with the logo of a Jakobstown trucking company, which I had found in one of the jet's lockers. My hair was a lot longer than it had been the last time I was on Reith, and at some point during my stay in the Dependencies I had grown a beard and hadn't bothered to shave it off. I already knew the rockers had long memories; I was about to find out just how accurate they were. "Unfortunately, Grandpa Raul is currently denying me access to his autodoc."

She shrugged. "We could have used mine."

I looked at her with renewed interest. "You've got one of those things?"

"Of course I have. Where have you been for the past – oh."

Exactly. While I had been wandering around the settled worlds, medical science had finally come up with the one device which could change my life, and I'd missed the event. I was going to have to buy one of the damn things. Which would mean buying a boat of my own to haul it around, and then it would just all get too fucking complicated again.

We rode out to Rockertown in a hovercraft piloted by one of Raul's descendants, a willowy young woman named Kelsey who had long auburn hair and regarded me with the expression of someone who had been carefully briefed beforehand by Sheldon. It wasn't a long trip, but I thought it was going to take a while before I stopped feeling Kelsey's glare on the back of my neck.

The landscape out here was an awesome flat expanse of reeds and sedge, through which water sparkled in the sunlight. The breeze on our faces smelled of rotting vegetation. All around us, *kopjes* rose up out of the Delta, some of them almost too small to stand on, others the size of office buildings. One of them, not too far away, was the one where we had buried JJ. I couldn't remember which particular rock it was, but I did remember that we'd had to use explosives to dig his grave and nobody had ever explained to me why we'd had to bury him there rather than in Jakobstown.

Kelsey piloted us down a cleared channel towards one huge rock, and as we got closer I saw the bulbous shapes of rocker houses arranged on it, and threads of smoke rising from their chimneys.

"They didn't all just wake up intelligent one morning," Suli said as we approached a wooden dock poking out into the marsh from the edge of Rockertown. "Their children are either born intelligent or not. There are still a lot of dumb rockers giving birth to smart children, and some smart rockers having dumb children."

"How do they feel about that?" I asked.

"They don't seem too bothered. They're not sentimental about the dumb rockers. They regard them as animals."

"What about the ones who have dumb children?"

"Same thing. As soon as the children are weaned they set them loose into the wild." She saw the look on my face and said, "They're not like us, Neil."

"You got *that* right."

"All I can tell you is we've never seen them hurt a dumb rocker. They're almost indifferent to them."

I sighed. I was going to hate every moment of this.

***

A welcome was waiting for us on the dock which stuck out into the water from the base of the rock. About a dozen rockers were standing patiently in line, watching us approach.

"That's the damndest thing I ever saw," I said, honestly astounded.

"They love to meet people," said Suli. "And they're so trusting." She sounded sad.

Kelsey cut the hovercraft's fans as we approached and we coasted to a stop beside the dock. Suli and I disembarked, and Kelsey fired up the engines again and roared off across the water, although not before giving me one last glare for good luck. I watched her go, then I took a deep breath and turned to face our reception committee.

Broadly-speaking, rockers looked like a misguided and inept attempt to genetically reengineer a giraffe. They stood about five feet tall at the shoulder, with a long muscular neck and a big head. They had six stout legs, but instead of hooves they had big flat four-toed feet and the front pair were slimmer and had hands with two opposed thumbs and three fingers. The last time I had seen a rocker, it had been using those hands to pull up marsh grasses and feed them between its big flat teeth. I had never seen a rocker do what these rockers were doing, which was hold up their right hands in unison and give us a little wave.

"Oh, crap," I murmured.

One of the rockers came up to us and Suli said, "Ringo, it's good to see you."

"It's good to see you too, Suli," said the rocker. It put out its hand and Suli shook it and I stared. Then it looked at me and held out its hand. "I presume you're Neil Hanson," it told me.

I kept staring.

"Shake his hand," Suli muttered out of the side of her mouth. "Let's not start off with a diplomatic incident."

I shook the rocker's hand. Its palm was velvety-soft, though the tips of its fingers and thumbs were rough and calloused. "Hi," I said in a small voice.

"Suli's been telling us all about you," said Ringo. It – he, it, whatever – was speaking perfectly bland American-accented English and its long neck put its head at about my eye-level. It blinked at me. "She says you came here with the first colonists, although you don't look nearly old enough."

Brilliant. Suli had told the rockers that we were colonists. Now all they had to do was decide that we were evil imperialist swine and take us to court and my life would be complete. I said, "I'm older than I look."

Ringo made an alarming snorting noise which was either laughter or meant that it was about to charge me. I took a step back and the rocker said, "Suli's explained the Push to us. But it's hard to understand."

"At any one time, only half a dozen people anywhere understand how the Push works," I said automatically. The rocker blinked at me. I blinked back.

"Well," it said. "I didn't say we *didn't* understand it. John McClaine's been working on the way the Bosworth-Goddard Transform applies to the Push."

"Fuck," I said, so quietly even I didn't hear it.

"He's discovering some quite promising results. Would you like to meet him?"

I shook my head slowly. "No..." I said. "No, that'll be...fine, thanks. Best not to...disturb him." I looked at Suli, who just shrugged almost imperceptibly.

Ringo suddenly rubbed its hands together. "Okay then," it said brightly, looking at both of us. "Let me show you round Rockertown."

***

Ringo and the rest of the rocker delegation led us up the steep street that wound up the side of the rock. It was in full tourist-guide mode, pointing out things of interest, like the artfully-woven huts, the little foundry that was smelting copper, a large hut that housed the rocker school, where a class of serious, studious young rockers was apparently learning about Brownian Motion, a rocker with a disastrously-uncombed mane sitting outside its hut and playing with a complicated frame of wires and beads that looked like a three-dimensional abacus. "John McClaine," Ringo said. I looked at Suli and she shrugged again.

Leaving aside a case of culture shock strong enough to rock me back on my heels and render me mute, there was no doubt about it. The rockers were an intelligent alien life form, the only one anybody had ever discovered. And we had hunted them almost to extinction.

After about an hour, I started to feel a bit better. Okay, the rockers were aliens, but apart from the fact of their intelligence there was nothing weird in Rockertown. Unless maybe you counted a rocker working on a theory of loop quantum gravity with the help of an abacus as *weird*. They had kids, and they taught their kids in schools, and they had a little police force and a distillery that made a spirit that was as close to 100% proof as made no difference. When I tasted the spirit I knew the rockers were just like us, and when they gave me a two-litre stoneware jug of the stuff, against Suli's admittedly weak protests ("No, it's all right, really, you don't have to do that, Mr Hanson doesn't drink. Really. Oh. All right, then.") I was their friend for life. All right-thinking sentient beings like alcohol.

I'd even stopped seeing them as rockers by the time we reached the crown of the rock. They'd learned everything they knew from us, from the language they used to the physics they were using. They were just funny-looking six-legged people. I'd taken a couple of drinks from the jug, as well, just to show how much I appreciated the gift. I'd even managed to swap a few jokes with Ringo and his deputy, Chester, although I'd had to explain mine.

"Will you *stop drinking?*" Suli said in an angry quiet voice. "You're making a fool of yourself."

"So would you," I muttered. "I know what comes next."

What came next was a ring of waist-high standing stones capping the very top of the rock like a crown, and at the centre of the ring a bigger rock.

"This is our God," Ringo said, and all the rockers made an abrupt and alarming lowing sound that I slowly realised was their own language. "Our stories tell of a giant devil who walked our land killing and eating us, until one day God came and defeated the devil. We carved this likeness of God to honour His memory."

I looked at the rock in the middle of the stone circle. I put the jug down at my feet.

"Of course," Ringo was saying, "many cultures have a

similar story in their early cosmology. I think it's a bunch of bullshit, myself. But some of the older people are comforted by it."

I stepped into the circle and walked up to the rock. I knelt down in front of it and there was some awed-sounding lowing from the rockers. I tipped my head to one side.

Raul was right, it *was* a pretty good likeness. It had a big nose and a weak mouth and a cleft chin. It looked, in other words, a lot like I had looked when I first came to Reith. Which raised all manner of questions about when precisely the rockers had started to become intelligent.

Suli walked up and stood beside me. "Go on," she said, too quietly for anybody else to hear, "perform a miracle."

I looked at the rockers and said, "I don't know why we're all worrying so much about the Agency; if the rockers remember *me* this well, they'll remember us hunting them. What we should *really* be worrying about is rocker lawyers taking us to court."

"They don't."

"Sorry?"

"They remember a demon giant hunting them. It's part of their creation myth. They don't connect it with us, any more than we blame snakes for being thrown out of Eden."

I got to my feet. "Let's go home."

***

Raul was waiting for us when we landed. He watched us walk from the plane and he said, "Oh, Christ, they didn't give him a jug of that white lightning, did they?"

"God is not drunk," I said, walking right past him towards the house. "But God wants the autodoc and woe betide anybody who gets in his way."

I heard his chair turn and follow me. "Neil...?"

"We are in all kinds of trouble," I told him without looking round or breaking stride. "God wants the autodoc. And then he wants to see Laura."

Four

Reith was not an aspirational kind of place, which was one of the reasons I liked it so much. Home's Continental Divide was modest by any standards. Its highest peaks appeared to have mustered the energy to raise their heads about three thousand metres above sea level and then just given up, which made them a landscape of alpine meadows in the Summer and a network of really great pistes in the Winter. There were only about four places along the Divide that would make an experienced climber look at them and think, `Yep, that looks quite difficult,' and of course Laura had decided to try and climb all of them.

Suli flew me to one of the little resorts in the valley at the foot of the mountain, then we took a cable-car up to a little hotel above the snowline. From the windows of the gondola, I watched snow-covered slopes and steeply-tilted forests and vertiginous rocky drops pass by and I listened to all the other passengers, with their brighly-coloured snowsuits and their skis and their snowboards and their snowgliders, chatting happily about the holidays they were having. Suli watched my face and didn't say anything.

At the hotel, we hired a snowmobile and motored a couple of kilometres slowly up empty trails overhung by trees so loaded with snow that they seemed to form a tunnel, until we broke out into bright sunlight in a deep little bowl cupped in the mountain's arms. Most of the bowl was hip-deep in snow, but towards the centre someone had come up from the hotel and cleared the snow away, revealing a patch of grass with a headstone sticking out of it. We parked the snowmobile at the edge of the clearing and waded through the snow until we reached the grass. Then we just stood there.

Eventually I said, "Was this for me?"

"Was what for you?" said Suli.

I waved a hand to indicate the cleared grass.

Suli smiled. "I think what you need to do is reassess how important you are."

"That's never been a problem before."

She laughed. "Someone comes up here every day during the winter and clears the snow away."

I looked at her. "After all this time?"

"After all this time."

I looked at her a few moments longer, then I walked across to the headstone and squatted down in front of it. There was new frost and snow on its face and I brushed a gloved hand across it to reveal the words LAURA HELEN MARCHMONT. That was all. That was all there ever had been. The stone looked a little more weathered than the last time I'd seen it.

After a while, Suli said, "You came back. I never understood that, really."

I knew what she was talking about. A year or so after Raul left me in the Dependencies and went back to Reith, I hired a boat and went back too. "It was more a case of second thoughts than a real change of mind," I said to the headstone.

"You must have known you'd never see her again, though."

"I didn't know *what* I was doing."

Silence, behind me. Then I heard the crunching of frost and thin snow on grass as Suli turned and walked towards the edge of the bowl and a view of plunging forests and snowfields and sunlit plains which was almost beyond description.

The boat I hired to take me back to Reith had better motors than *Mason*'s upgrade, and I arrived about ten years after Raul got back from the Dependencies, much to his annoyance. The colony had swollen beyond recognition with new arrivals. I hadn't expected Laura to still be there, but in my dark heart I suppose I did really. We had good medical facilities, the suspension tanks on *Dixon* had still been in orbit when we left. I thought she'd be waiting for me to change my mind.

Instead, what she did was have three children and two failed marriages. She decided to climb the only four tough walls on Reith, working north to south. The first two were simple. The third, a wall about twice the height of El Capitan, took almost a week of hard work. She fell off the fourth, a pissy climb she could have done in her sleep.

I stood up and brushed snow off my knees and looked around the bowl. The last time I'd seen this place had been in the summer and I was in shorts and shirtsleeves and the grass in the meadow was full of little star-shaped beige flowers. I'd spent half an hour or so wondering what in Christ I was doing there, then I'd hiked back down to the foot of the mountain – this was long before the cable-car – and flown back to Jakobstown, where Raul was the father of twins and had just been elected Planetary Commissioner, which I always thought was a pretty fancy title for the man everyone in the world whines to if something goes wrong with their lives. Then I'd got on the first boat that was leaving the system and I just kept going until I got Raul's email.

***

The vast percentage of the populace – 'the wee folk,' JJ called them – have no idea just how much money it's possible for one person to have. Everyone can get their mind around the idea of being a millionaire, and quite a lot of people can cope with the concept of being a billionaire. But after that, well, it's all just numbers, the sort of money that big faceless corporations have, not relatively ordinary individuals.

Having said that, none of us ever had any idea of what it was like to be poor. Or just ordinarily rich. Or even relatively well-off. It was just impossible to visualise. We thought of ourselves as ordinary people, just with bigger dreams. Back in the old days, when we were still having theoretical discussions about what we would do with all our money and JJ still hadn't had the Big Idea, Raul added up our combined worth and declared that between us we could afford to buy Illinois, an idea that I was quite taken with. For a while I fantasised about renaming Chicago 'Hansonburg,' but then JJ got interested in the Push and we all just lost our minds to the idea of colonising Outer Space, and that was when we and the United Nations Space Agency wound up on a collision course.

The Agency hated private enterprise. If they'd had their way, our operation would have been closed down the moment we bought *Mason* and *Dixon*. The Agency felt that the best way to colonise the Galaxy was to pussy around in meetings, agonising about the impact on native environments. If you printed out their colonisation protocols, they'd fill the Library of Congress two or three times over. Agency colonies tended to be established on worlds with the bare minimum of native life, and were consequently some of the grimmest places in the known universe.

On the other hand, we had landed on Reith, turned it into a Garden of Eden, and gone quite a long way towards exterminating an intelligent species. I could almost hear the Agency's lawyers sharpening their knives.

Putting together a colony project is still enormously expensive, but in the early days it was *apocalyptically* expensive. Back then there were probably only half a dozen or so individuals and organisations who could have managed it, and only the Agency and us four were crazy enough to actually try it.

We took the Agency by surprise with Pictoris, but they didn't stay surprised for too long. We were still on our way to Reith when they got their act together, taking their case to the UN Special Court in Dushanbe in an operation the like of which had not been seen since D-Day. As this was a UN court, they of course won, and a resolution was passed into UN law forbidding private colonies. We were all criminals when we landed on Reith, but by then it was too late to stop us.

It was John-Jakob who had the Idea. It was always JJ who had the Idea. He sat the rest of us down one night in one of *Mason*'s dropships, on the bank of the Slow River, where Jakobstown would one day become a bustling metropolis, and he spelled it out for us.

It was perfectly simple, the way he saw it. We could pack the colony up and go home with our tails between our legs. In which case the colonists would sue us, and we would be reduced to penury. *Or* we could establish the colony and go home. In which case the UNSA would keep us in the courts for the rest of our lives, then take all our money. *Or* we could declare Reith a sovereign entity and secede from the UN.

I think that it was me who laughed when he suggested that.

That, more or less, was the point at which everything started to fall apart for us. We argued for weeks, often in very loud voices, and sometimes we argued in front of the colonists, which did morale no good at all. I wanted no part of a ruck with the Agency; we were mind-bogglingly rich, but compared to the

Agency we were still little people, and the little people lose every time. I wanted to cut a deal, to get out with some portion of my money intact, and to go live somewhere uneventful, like Sweden. Laura sided with JJ, and nothing I could do would persuade her otherwise. Raul, bless him, resisted all arguments and sat on the fence.

In the end, it was the colonists who decided things for us. While we'd been debating geopolitics, they'd been facing the somewhat starker choice between trying to survive and waiting to see what we would do. They'd decided to try and survive. Reith had become a colonised world, and it was going to stay that way.

So, we emailed the Agency and told them to fuck off. We invoked Free Enterprise. We invoked the Boston Tea Party. We invoked the Belt Secession Act. We invoked the Declaration of Independence. We may also have invoked Magna Carta and the song of the Mickey Mouse Club, I don't remember. I was drunk most of the time. And we got away with it.

I still don't really understand what happened. Maybe only JJ understood it properly, and some of the Agency lawyers he negotiated with. I could ask the Agency, I suppose, but there wouldn't be any point, and they probably wouldn't want to talk to me anyway.

What *seemed* to happen was that the UNSA rolled over on its back and let us rub its tummy. We seceded from the UN, then we signed about a thousand treaties, and at the end of it all we wound up with a fully-functioning, independent colony, with a seat on the UN Security Council and too many trading agreements for my small brain to accommodate. The negotiations overwhelmed the colony qubit transceiver's entanglement lattice and we had to use the one from the boats.

At which point, and shouting dire warnings at anyone who seemed to be halfway interested, I got the hell out of Dodge. I didn't trust the Agency. I knew they were just waiting to fuck us over in some way we hadn't thought of. So I lit out for the Dependencies. Left everyone behind to face the coming storm.

***

We were not the only people to settle Reith. Even before we got there more colonists were on their way, all licenced through our company, and when word got back about how pleasant the place was the floodgates just opened. Every year boats carrying thousands, tens of thousands, arrived, and while Raul was still on his way back from dropping me off in the Dependencies the *UNSAS William Jefferson Clinton* entered orbit, a boat carved from a rock the size of Ireland and carrying over three quarters of a million colonists in suspension. We had had our differences, but the Agency knew a good thing when they saw it. Their own colonies were awful howling wildernesses that no one in their right mind would want to live on. Ditto Mars, which after three centuries of terraforming still sucked. They signed a contract with us, spent the next fifteen years building and fitting out the *Clinton*, then they filled it with anybody who wanted to leave overcrowded Earth, and sent them on their way. We made…oh, I don't know, we made an *obscene* amount of money out of the deal.

The *Clinton* made four trips to Reith, each time with more efficient motors, before Raul put a cap on immigration. Not because there wasn't room for everybody but because it was just getting harder and harder to keep track of the new folks, for some of whom the pioneering spirit which led them to leave Earth in the first place expressed itself in new and interesting ways when they arrived on Reith. Such as setting up their own countries – surprisingly often with governments based on the Divine Right of Kings – on some of the less-settled islands. Raul frowned on megalomania, and some Police Actions had been necessary.

I watched all this from a varying but still considerable distance as I did my three-year swing through the Settled Worlds. I shook my head at the news feeds I saw on Nowa Polska. I tutted at the stories I read in a newspaper on Weiss Heim. I believe I may have chuckled out loud at a magazine article I saw on Daybreak. I kept moving, boat to boat to boat. Time passed. After more than two centuries, real-time, the project that I had thought would be a mildly diverting adventure, a bit of a giggle, had become a planet with twenty-four and a half million inhabitants. I still didn't know how I felt about that.

Five

Suli and I spent weeks in Rockertown, but I never visited the statue again. We talked with Ringo and his friends. I got drunk with a bunch of rocker yobs and taught them about graffiti and Suli shouted at me. I was arrested and spent a night in Rockertown's jail, a hut of woven grass I could have cut my way out of with a rusty penknife. We flew Ringo to Raul's estate and we sat him down and explained what was going on. We told him what the stakes were. I demonised the Agency as much as it was possible without flat-out telling him they were a bunch of devils. Then we flew him back to Rockertown to talk to his people. Maybe *they* could come up with some ideas.

At the end of the Summer we had what Raul described as a council of war, although a disinterested observer might have described it as a bloody good dinner followed by drinks and cigars in the study. In this regard it wasn't very much different from all the other dinners we'd had at Raul's house over the past few months, followed by brainstorming sessions which went on well into the early hours of the next morning and usually resulted in me standing with my arm in the autodoc for stringently-enforced treatment periods.

We were all aware, however, that time was getting short. Raul had been receiving increasingly-stern emails from the Agency asking for updates about the rockers; he was also keeping a close eye on about thirty recent arrivals and a hundred older colonists he suspected of being undercover Agency operatives. He wasn't annoyed about this; it was just the way things worked. He had his own sources scattered around the Settled Worlds, and any day now one of them was going to tip him off that the Agency had decided to move against us.

"So how long do you think we'll have once they set out?" he asked.

"The Dependencies are their nearest jump-off point," Sheldon said smoothly. "With the new generation motors that's three months flight time, about a year objective."

Raul looked at me, and I sighed. Everybody else thought the Agency would do the obvious thing and come at us from their nearest base, but the Agency was like an ageing starlet looking for one last big production, and I knew they'd launch a mission from Earth under the full glare of publicity. We wouldn't need Raul's spies; we'd read about it on the news feeds, and three years later the Agency would be here. I tipped my glass at Raul to remind him of all this, and he gave me a long-suffering look.

"How long would it take them if they left from the place you came from?" he asked.

He never forgot, never gave up. I smiled and shook my head. I hadn't been terribly far away when I got his email asking for help, but the people there had good reason for wanting to keep their whereabouts quiet and I had agreed not to tell anybody about them. I'd had to make a detour to The Dependencies to pick up my ride on the *Wednesday Addams*, rather than travel to Reith direct, and now I thought about it I had to wonder whether any interested parties might have noticed me passing through, and if they had whether they'd try to find out where I'd come from.

I stood up. "I'll be back in a minute."

"Sit down, Neil," said Raul.

"I've got to –"

"Whatever damage has been done has already been done," he said. "It'll wait till morning."

He had, of course, known exactly where I was when I heard from him. "It might not."

He shook his head. "Sit down, Neil."

I sat, wondering if people over the age of a hundred and seventy suddenly became telepathic and clairvoyant. I said, "Do you do telekinesis as well?" and Raul laughed, but I was really going to have to send an email tomorrow.

"What we really need is JJ," Raul said. "JJ was never short of ideas."

"Which is why we're in this fucking mess in the first place," I said. "John-Jakob and all his fucking ideas."

Suli and Sheldon looked shocked to hear someone speak thus about the sainted Commander Reith. Sod them; they never knew what an unbearable smartarse John-Jakob could be.

In retrospect, I was probably more annoyed than I should have been, but I said, "Maybe it's time you kids put your history books away. JJ was a total jerk." More shocked looks. "Oh, for Christ's sake, he wasn't even a *Commander*. He never went *near* the military. It would have been too much like hard work. He just called himself *Commander* because he piloted *Dixon* out here."

"Actually, he didn't even do that," said Raul.

We all looked at him.

He shrugged. "He had no more idea how to pilot a Push boat than I have how to make an elephant levitate. He hired a guy to fly *Dixon* and then told everybody he did it himself."

Suli's and Sheldon's mouths were hanging open. I found myself smiling beatifically. "I didn't know that."

"Sure," he said. "Remember Norman Czerniak?"

"Stormin' Norman? Of course I do." Raul was forgetting that, as far as I was concerned, I'd last seen Stormin' Norman less than five years ago. We'd signed up thirty crew for each boat, whose duties involved little more than spending a few days every other month out of suspension during the trip looking after the boat systems and helping us unload the colony at the other end, in return for a massive discount on the fare to Reith. Norman Czerniak had been one of *Dixon*'s crew, a cheerful, almost-spherical Polish American whose personal baggage allowance had consisted of thirty cases of Zubrowka vodka and a small suitcase of jumpsuits, Hawaiian shirts and underwear. Norman and I had had some good times... "*Norman* flew *Dixon*? How did they get away with that?"

"I don't imagine it was difficult. Almost everybody was in suspension, just the rotating caretaker crew up and about, you remember how it was. They just made sure they were both out of suspension at the same times, made sure none of the caretakers were on the bridge when Norman was doing piloting stuff. JJ paid him six million Swiss francs to do the flying and keep his mouth shut. Made him sign a contract."

"Jesus." I sat back and thought about it. You could teach a bright kid to pilot a Push boat, and it had simply been too much trouble for JJ to learn. He'd been dead two hundred years and he was still surprising me. "How come *you* know about it?"

"After JJ died and you left, Norman read his contract again and decided he ought to tell *somebody*. He couldn't stand it here and he was getting ready to go home with the second wave of colony boats. He came to see me one night and we drank some of his baggage allowance, and he told me."

"And you told him not to repeat this to anybody else."

"I looked over his contract and I told him that if he wanted any of that money to be waiting for him when he got back to Earth, he'd better *not* repeat it to anybody else." He looked innocently at us. "What? It was just common-sense advice."

"Devious little bastard," I muttered, shaking my head. But Raul was right: JJ would have been here right now, full of ideas, if I hadn't killed him.

We all sat around the table in silence, looking at each other or at the remains of our meal or into space. I was angry. The Agency was coming to try and take our planet away from us, and when they found that the rockers were intelligent there would be nothing to stop them. I couldn't prevent the Agency sending people here. Bribery – and I was in a position to hand out in bribes sums of money previously unthought-of in human history – might put off the inevitable for a while, but that would only convince people we had something to hide.

I was just mentally trying to tot up how much it would cost to have the whole UNSA top brass assassinated when something else occurred to me.

I said, "How far does your influence reach, Raul?"

"Outside this system? Oh, I don't known. It probably wouldn't be beyond me to get a short-order chef fired for undercooking my meal." He looked at me. "Here, I have the power of life and death. Are you starting to get an idea?"

I wasn't sure yet, but I'd just thought of something that was so weird that the Agency would *have* to believe it.

I said, "Can you lay your hands on a couple of colony boats? Without anyone finding out about it?" And then I sat there, wondering why Raul and Suli and Sheldon were laughing.

***

The whole Reith solar system was a modest sort of place. Two rocky planets, one habitable, one not. Four moderately-sized gas giants, not too complicated for scoop mining. And an unassuming asteroid belt. Which, since I had last visited, was larger by two rocks.

Sheldon and I ascended to The Hook, then he revealed a hitherto unsuspected talent and piloted us out to the asteroid belt in a little intrasystem tug.

"I told Grandfather to get rid of them," Sheldon said as he manoeuvred the tug towards a potato-shaped asteroid about thirty klicks long. "But he wouldn't hear of it. He said he wanted to set up a museum out here one day."

I watched the rock grow larger on the tug's dashboard screens. "And nobody else knows they're here."

He shook his head. "Nobody knows, nobody cares. I come out here once a month to run a system check."

As we got closer, I could see a ring of blisters circling the rock's midsection where the Push motors had been installed. I knew that inside there were kilometres of corridors, holds the size of sports arenas, caverns lined with suspension tanks. Swooping low over the surface, I saw the word *DIXON* carved into the rock in letters hundreds of metres long. On the tug's orbital plotter, a little orange dot marked where *Mason* was, about a thousand kilometres away.

"We'll have to refuel the insystem drives," I said. "Without anyone knowing about it."

"Shouldn't be a problem," he said. "We run a hydrogen mining station around Cyndi." Another ex-wife, this time donating her name to one of the system's gas giants. "The problem is what to do about the personnel who get it here and do the refuelling."

"We'll do it ourselves," I said. "Keep the number of outsiders to a minimum. Then we kill everyone else." Silence, from Sheldon. "Joke," I told him.

"It better be," he said.

"You know," I said, "we might be able to do this."

He grunted. "I think you're crazy, myself."

"You have a better idea?"

"No," he said.

"All right then," I said smugly. "Let's do this thing. And let's all keep our fingers crossed too."

Six

John-Jakob was an arsehole. He was very bright, very handsome, very popular, but he was still an arsehole, and when Laura said she was going to stay on Reith with him, I conceived a particularly bitter hatred.

John-Jakob didn't realise, of course. Clever, popular, good-looking arseholes can never understand that some people might not like them.

So when he suggested a flight out to the Delta he just thought it would be a bit of fun. That was a few days after our final argument and my declaration that I was leaving, so I know he was justifying it to himself as some way of talking me out of going. But really this was just a bit of a jaunt. And along the way we could shoot a few rockers and he could show me where he was planning to site Jakobstown's reactor. That was the way JJ's mind worked: kill some animals, persuade Neil not to leave, and demonstrate how clever he was. He just didn't realise that the person he was having his jaunt with was the one person on the planet who hated him more than anyone else within several hundred light years.

He showed me where his reactor would be. It was far enough from human habitation that if anything went catastrophically wrong the colonists would be safe. We trudged for hours across little muddy islands and through sedge, waist-deep in stinking water. John-Jakob killed a couple of rockers, but I was too angry to concentrate on hunting. He'd been up for four straight days swapping emails with the Agency's lawyers, finalising the agreements that would ensure Reith's independence and he was babbling on and on about his stupid plans and it was driving me crazy. I kept thinking of him and Laura sitting side by side at our last conference, holding hands the whole time. He was really starting to annoy me.

We wound up on one of the big rocks. We climbed to the top, and John-Jakob *still* wouldn't stop reeling off his fucking ideas. He was like some minor god, pointing here and there and telling me what he wanted to be here and there and, because he was John-Jakob and the fucking *planet* was named after him, it would come to pass.

He was standing at the edge of the rock at this point, and I just walked over to him and pushed. He didn't cry out. He just went over the edge; one moment there, next moment not. It wasn't a particularly long fall, but he fell head-first, and I'll never forget the sound he made when he landed.

I don't know how long I stood there looking down at his body lying on the rocks below me. I remember, however, that when I turned round to go back to the jet half a dozen rockers were standing looking at me. I waved my arms at them, and they turned away and wandered off like the mindless animals they were...

Except they weren't quite mindless animals, even then. They remembered seeing *something*, and they told their children, and their children told *their* children, and somehow – telepathy, race memory, whatever – they had passed on my likeness as well, and by the time Raul contacted me the rockers thought they had seen God casting down the Devil.

Everyone believed me when I told them John-Jakob had slipped and fallen. Reith was still a frontier world; it was still too easy to die in a stupid accident. John-Jakob went into history as the man who had given his life to colonise Reith. He wasn't the only person to die, of course, but History's like that. He was *the* man.

And the only ones who knew the truth were the rockers. And instead of telling anyone, they just made me their God.

***

It turned out that the reactor John-Jakob told me about on the day I killed him was built with a design fault. It was one of those tiny, stupid, unforeseen design faults that don't matter very much if they're built into, say, a bath tap or the windscreen washer of your car. But after running for almost two hundred years it finally failed and caused a disaster several orders of magnitude larger than Chernobyl. The prevailing winds blew an unbelievably radioactive plume of steam and vaporised debris across the Rocker preserve, where rains carried it to the ground.

The rockers all died, in horrifying agony. The area was made uninhabitable for the next thousand years. Raul sent us pictures of the dying rockers and they were hard to look at. We were, as it turned out, only just in time. As we left, news came through that the Agency was sending a cruiser to Reith packed to the airlocks with investigators.

"We'll take some lumps, of course," said Raul. "They're going to make our lives hell for letting the rockers die in the accident, but the evidence of their intelligence is gone so we should be able to ride it out. It's going to be up to the lawyers."

He looked around his study. "Have I left anything out? Oh, yes. My doctors tell me I'm too old and sick for the Agency to use truth drugs on me, and my condition will probably screw up the results of a polygraph test. My lawyers say I'll be able to refuse anything more than a light interview on those grounds. I'll be in touch." He leaned forward and his image vanished from the screen.

"He's dead now," Sheldon said beside me.

I did the sums. "Maybe not."

Sheldon snorted.

I unfastened my seat harness. "Don't underestimate him," I told him. "I wouldn't bet on him not being at Point B waiting for us." I kicked out of my seat and into the corridor.

Sheldon was right, though. We'd been on our way for a couple of months now. If you factored in the time dilation of *Mason*'s and *Dixon*'s old Push motors, almost twenty years had passed on Reith. Which meant that we had already either got away with it, or been found out.

Instead of using a qubit transceiver – which would have retained records of its transmission and would have been one of the first things an Agency search squad looked for – Raul had beamed his message along our course using an enormous laser a bunch of scientists had built as part of an experiment in the system's cometary halo. Anyone approaching Reith from this direction would pick up the message pretty easily, but the cute thing was that, apart from the early Agency flyby probe, nobody had ever *seen* the system from the outside. Certainly we never did; all traffic dropped out of the Push well within the orbit of Cyndi, and I presumed whoever was handling Raul's transmissions was making sure there were no records. Still, it was undeniably spooky. Raul was probably the toughest person I'd ever met, but nobody lives for ever. And I was going to keep getting messages from him for years to come, while we ambled towards Point B.

Mason and *Dixon*. The colony boats were just old asteroids hung between Push motors and wormed with kilometres of corridors. The corridors were empty right now because most of our cargo was in suspension in the four big caverns at *Mason*'s heart. I went hand over hand down them, along a line of grab-loops, until I reached a big spherical room full of computer equipment and control panels and hologram displays and acceleration couches. Some of the couches had been hurriedly adapted to hold people who were not human, and one of them was occupied.

"And?" asked Ringo.

I settled into my couch and strapped in. "As of the last dispatch, we might still have got away with it."

Ringo sighed and flipped a couple of switches. "The suspense is killing me," he said.

"Try and put yourself in Raul's shoes," I told him. "The Agency's not the gentlest of organisations."

It had not, of course, taken long to teach the rockers how to operate the boats' systems. They had taken to freefall as if born to it, and although most of the ten thousand or so we had brought with us were in suspension, around a hundred had volunteered to join the caretaking crew.

Out of the corner of my eye, I saw Sheldon and Suli drift through the control room, hand in hand. Suli hadn't spoken to me since long before we left Reith. She'd tried to veto the plan and been voted down, then had announced she wanted nothing to do with it, then had announced that she was going to come with us anyway because somebody had to be on board who had the rockers' best interests at heart. I watched them go through one of the doors on the other side of the room. They were holding hands a lot these days, I'd noticed. Sheldon was really starting to annoy me.

As well as the ten thousand smart rockers, evacuated from

various places around Reith, we were carrying about seven thousand dumb rockers and everyone who had ever been connected with their rise to intelligence. Most of these were members of Raul's extended family, who regarded him as somewhere between God and Santa Claus and would have gone anywhere and done anything he told them. Basically, we had put together a big gang, stolen the evidence, and then run away with it.

I was hoping it was weird and unlikely enough for the Agency not to guess what we'd done. Somewhere in suspension we had an entire movie industry special-effects crew, who had furnished us with the horrible footage of dying rockers, but we had needed to leave physical evidence behind as well, so we really had blown up the reactor, and we had left a large number of dumb rockers on the reservation to die of radiation poisoning so there would be remains for the Agency to examine, which was where Suli and I parted company. She accused me of genocide and hadn't said a word to me since.

Ringo saw me watching her leave the control room and said, "Eventually, she'll realise you did the right thing."

I looked at him. "You think?"

"Sure," he said. "*We* all think you did the right thing. If we'd stayed on Reith the Agency would have taken the planet over and we'd have wound up being poked and prodded by every scientist they've got. This way, we're free and on our way to a great adventure."

"Suli doesn't quite see it that way."

"She will. Give her time."

"Well," I said, "at least we have plenty of *that*."

Seven

We approached Point B carefully, dropping out of the Push well outside the limit of the system's Oort Cloud and deploying sensor drones to give us a long baseline to look and listen insystem. The drones picked up the light of fusion drives and heard radio communications. There were people here.

Which was not unexpected. We were facing the same problem Raul and JJ and Laura and I had faced when we first set out all those years ago – that someone with a more efficient Push drive would get there first. This time, I *knew* there were more efficient drives; everyone else had them, and I could only presume that they would keep on getting better.

When we left Reith, Point B's survey had only just been released onto the Agency's database. It was a little world with a Reithtype atmosphere and it was going through the mother and father of all ice ages, but there was a chunky little temperate zone around the equator that we could live in. I was gambling that Point B was such an unpromising colony prospect that nobody would bother settling it, but that had been almost two hundred years ago, realtime, and clearly I had been wrong.

In *Dixon*'s holds we were carrying, among other things, four small Push boats. We unshipped one and sent a couple of people insystem posing as reps for a freight agency. In between scaring up business for outsystem haulage they established that the trust I had moved all my money into was still running, and they came back with qubit lattices and an update for the survey database and terabytes of new technical specs and whole libraries of recorded media. Basically, we were catching up on civilisation.

Point B – the colonists called it Ola – was a thriving little world governed by a benign theocracy and had just begun construction work on its own skyhook. Fashions and entertainments were frankly baffling. The Agency was now the most powerful organisation on Earth, the *de facto* government, really, which annoyed me immensely. The Settled Worlds were now known as 'Human Space,' which also annoyed me. Of Reith, there was not a single mention anywhere on Ola's newsnets. Encyclopaedia entries showed a still-independent Reith, with a population of well over a hundred million, and not a word about the rockers. Maybe we'd got away with it. Maybe the Agency knew all about what we'd done but couldn't prove it. Maybe, maybe…

We hung about for a few months, far out in the dark, going through the new database for candidates for Point C, but I wasn't unduly worried. If Point C turned out to be inhabited when we got there, we could always go on to Points D, E and F. We had food synthesisers and suspension and a scoop-tanker squirreled away in one of *Dixon*'s holds to mine hydrogen fuel from gas giants. We were going to creep through the night between the stars and, in all likelihood, we were all going to live a very very long time. We could outrun the Agency, if we kept going long enough. We might even wind up outliving it, and I liked that idea very much.

Raul, being Raul, had of course known all along exactly what the solution to the problem was. But he had also known that he would never be able to do it, that he would never be able to run away from Reith. That was why he had called me. Running away had never been a problem for me.

Finally, we found a good prospect for our next destination and turned away from Ola, up and out into the night, and we kept running.